# FATAL CONNECTION

## FROM THE OUTER REACHES ...

Fatal Connection
by Malcolm Rose

Published by Ransom Publishing Ltd.
Unit 7, Brocklands Farm, West Meon, Hampshire GU32 1JN, UK
www.ransom.co.uk

ISBN        978 178127 671 6
First published in 2015

Printed and bound in Great Britain by Clays Ltd, St Ives plc

# FATAL CONNECTION

## MALCOLM ROSE

Ransom

**By the same author**

**From The Outer Reaches ...**

## BODY HARVEST

*When the body of an outer is discovered in the woods, young detective Troy Goodhart and forensic specialist Lexi Iona Four are partnered on the case. Then two more bodies are discovered, and all three corpses are found to have body parts missing. Somebody is killing with a purpose. As major Troy and outer Lexi unpick the case, they enter a complex, dark world of deception, where one false move will mean death.*

## LETHAL OUTBREAK

*Three scientists wearing airtight protective suits are found dead in a sealed, high-security laboratory. They had been studying an unknown substance brought to Earth by the recently returned Mars probe. Was this substance responsible for their deaths? Was it an accident — or could it be murder? Young detective Troy Goodhart and forensic specialist Lexi Iona Four quickly realise that this case is about something much worse than straightforward murder.*

# THE OUTER REACHES

*A world inhabited by two distinct and non-interbreeding humanoid species: **majors** (the majority) and **outers**. The two races are outwardly similar, but they have different talents, different genetics and different body chemistry.*

*In this world, meet major Troy Goodhart and outer Lexi Iona Four. They make an amazing crime-fighting partnership.*

# SCENE 1

*Thursday 1st May, Afternoon*

Richard groaned and pushed his aching body up onto one elbow. He coughed violently and his chest exploded with pain. When he wiped his mouth with his left hand, his forefinger came away wet and glistening red. His pillow was stained the same colour and small clumps of his hair were matted onto the material.

He reached out towards his bedside cabinet, but hesitated as his tongue explored inside his mouth. Shaking, he slid two fingers past the blue line on his gum and poked at one particular tooth. Without resistance, it came away. For several seconds, he gazed in horror at the large molar in his hand. His tongue told him it wasn't the only wobbly one.

He didn't know what was happening to him, but it was clearly more than an upset stomach after eating something bad or drinking too much beer. His instinct told him that it was already too late to call for help, but he still wanted his phone.

He dropped the tooth on the duvet and stretched out his left arm towards his mobile. His vision swirled as if he were still drunk and his coordination failed him. He tried to snatch up the phone but he missed. He leaned over the edge of the bed and vomited. He waited for the world to stop spinning and gulped down the bile in his mouth. Suspecting that he had swallowed another tooth, he tried again.

His fingertips bashed into the mobile and pushed it against the lamp. There, he managed to scoop it up, but he fell off his elbow. Lying flat on his back, he held his phone above his face and tried to tap the screen in the right places. There was something he had to do for the sake of his family.

Salty drops ran down his cheeks and the sheet underneath him was wet with sweat. He cursed his inability to see straight and the wild trembling of his fingers, completely out of his control. The room seemed unnaturally quiet. But he guessed that the background noise was normal. His ears felt like they were stuffed with cotton wool. A toenail snagged on the duvet and detached painlessly from his foot.

On the shelf opposite his bed there was an old-fashioned mercury thermometer. From where he lay, he couldn't make out the reading. It was probably perfect. No doubt, it was his body chemistry that was making him hot.

It wasn't just the tremors and numbness of his hands that frustrated him. He was having trouble making sense of the phone's screen and symbols. He couldn't remember what they meant and what to do with them. His mind was muddled.

Richard was glad that his wife and children were not at home to witness his dreadful state. When they'd left early this morning, he'd had a lousy headache, some nausea and dizziness. Blaming it on a hangover, they hadn't had a lot of sympathy for him. But as the day wore on, he had not perked up. Feeling more and more miserable, he'd stayed in bed. Now, his stomach churned as he realized that his body was in serious meltdown.

Nervously, his fumbling fingers clawed at the screen of his phone. Somehow, he had accessed the settings. Grimly determined, he scanned down the list of options. The letters and words drifted in and out of focus. His forehead creased with concentration and bemusement. Then he saw it. *Return to factory settings.*

He mumbled out loud, 'Yes.' Desperately trying to limit the shivering of his hands, he touched the box on the screen. The phone asked him, *Are you sure? This function erases all data on phone.* 'Yes,' he said again. Even if his phone had accepted voice input, it might not have recognized that croak. He tapped the link and nothing happened because he missed the target. He tried again. This time, he hit the spot.

*Resetting.*

At least now his wife would be spared his recent behaviour. He owed her that.

His arms flopped heavily onto the bed. His phone fell onto his chest and then slithered off his shoulder. Richard no longer had the strength to put it back on the bedside cabinet. He lay there, stranded, ashamed, bewildered, barely able to breath.

Soon, he would not even be able to manage that.

# SCENE 2

*Sunday 4th May, Morning*

In Shepford, one hundred kilometres north of Richard Featherstone's house, Dr Miriam Thirteen looked down at her patient and shook her head. 'I'm old enough to remember dancing cats.'

Standing on the other side of the bed, the young medical trainee frowned. 'Sorry?'

Miriam Thirteen nodded at the bloodied major girl lying between them. The sedatives had made her comfortable and quiet but, when she'd been admitted to the hospital, her body had been totally out of control. 'All the tremors and twitching. Like wild jittery dancing.'

'You mentioned cats.'

'Yes. It was a time when people – and factories – weren't so careful about pollution. Heavy metals – things like lead, mercury and cadmium – got everywhere. They were in paint, petrol, light bulbs and all sorts. And in the environment. They caused this sort of damage. The local cats used to get poisoned with the metals and lose control of their extremities. A lot of people called it dancing cat fever.' The elderly doctor sighed. 'I haven't seen a case for years.'

'You think it's heavy-metal poisoning?'

She nodded. 'If I remember rightly, it's down to mercury. The blue line on her gum, loose teeth, nails and hair, red fingers and toes, confusion and sickness. Yes. And I don't think we can wait for the toxicity results to confirm it, or we won't have a patient to treat.'

'Is there an antidote?'

'Dimercaptosuccinic acid – DMSA. Or activated charcoal. Even if I'm right, I don't know what type of mercury she's contaminated with. I'll administer both, but … It depends how long it's been in her body, how much of it there is, and what damage it's already done to her kidneys and central nervous system. A high concentration of mercury – or a long exposure – is irreversible for a major.'

Dr Miriam Thirteen and the trainee were not like their patient. They belonged to the other human species. They were both outers.

Miley Quist was unaware of the two doctors and her surroundings. She wasn't aware of her rapidly deteriorating health. She didn't even notice the frantic attempts to mop up the mercury from her poisoned body with medicines. She died fifty days before her fifteenth birthday.

# SCENE 3

## Monday 5th May, Morning

Terabyte blew the dust off the lens of his glasses and repositioned them on his nose. 'It's a program I wrote when I first came here,' he said to Lexi Four, Troy Goodhart and the chief of police at Shepford Crime Central. 'I knew it'd be useful one day. It collects all the information on deaths nationwide. It alerts me as soon as it sees too many deaths – above the expected average – in a particular area. It could be a doctor making mistakes, or even murdering patients. It highlights the hotspot. Good for flagging up a failing doctor or a serial killer before it gets out of hand. It also looks at causes of death and tips me off about any unusual ones.'

'Very interesting,' the commander said. He hesitated and then asked, 'Do you have a name?'

Shepford Crime Central's best computer geek smiled. 'Yes, but you can call me Terabyte – like everyone else. I like it.'

'So, what have you brought us here to see? What's making alarm bells go off?'

Terabyte took a handful of his hair and shoved it behind his ear. 'A few strange ones pop up now and again. Deaths, I mean.' He shrugged. 'Probably doesn't mean anything apart from bad luck. But how about three strange deaths with identical causes at more-or-less the same time?'

Detective Lexi Iona Four replied, 'I don't believe in that much bad luck – or coincidence.'

'What are these unusual deaths?' the commander asked impatiently.

'Mercury poisoning.'

'Mercury?'

'Yes. So it says on the death certificates. All within a week. Richard Featherstone, Keaton Hathaway and Miley Quist. And when I searched on symptoms, I think there's another one – Alyssa Bending – put down to unknown causes on Friday.'

'Weird,' said Detective Troy Goodhart. 'Where are they?'

'That's interesting and unusual as well,' Terabyte replied. 'Miley Quist was here in Shepford. She died last night. The other three are all over the place. North and south of here. None of them are within a hundred kilometres of each other.'

'So, what's the connection?'

Terabyte shrugged. 'You're the detectives.'

'These deaths,' the chief said, 'they're all majors.'

Lexi told him, 'Mercury doesn't affect outers. Well, not unless they take ridiculously huge amounts. The liquid metal doesn't affect majors either. You can stick your finger in it and whirl it around. Good fun. Nothing will happen. But its compounds and mercury vapour are very different. They pass straight through outers, but they're super-toxic to majors.' She glanced down at the information on her laptop. 'Nasty symptoms. Not a nice way to go.'

'Don't get all technical with me,' the commander replied. 'I don't have the time.' He glanced at the three teenage police officers, one after the other, and came to a decision. 'Okay. Look into it. It's your next case.' He got up and walked out.

'Well, thanks, Terabyte,' Lexi said with a smile. 'You've got us another wacky one.'

'My pleasure,' he replied with a smirk.

Troy said, 'Top of the list: what's the connection?'

Lexi laughed. 'They're majors – probably in some strange religious sect that worships mercury. At least it exists, unlike other things majors worship.'

Religion came easily to majors, but outers like Lexi and Terabyte rarely believed in anything but facts.

'Right,' Troy replied. 'Your best guess is a meeting of a cult that adores a shiny metal. I'll trump that. Maybe they've all eaten the same contaminated food.'

Becoming serious, Lexi said, 'Or drink.'

'How about this? They've all been to the same place. Somewhere that's been poisoned.'

Lexi nodded. 'Or they've all upset the same person – who's now getting his or her revenge.'

'Maybe they've all taken the same bad batch of pills,' Troy suggested.

'That's a good idea. I'm sure there's a medicine or something that's got mercury in it. I'll look it up.'

'I'm beginning to struggle now,' Troy admitted. 'I think we've got the obvious ones. But … here's a long shot. They could've all come into contact with contaminated animals – ones that get around a lot. Like birds.' He shrugged and then grinned at Lexi. 'I feel one of your spreadsheets coming on,' he said.

'Yeah. I'll definitely build something that'll make it easy to spot links. We'll see.'

'If I wanted to murder someone using mercury,' Troy said, 'where would I get it from?'

Lexi tapped at her keypad. 'It's used in industry for making chlorine, cement, caustic soda and sulphuric acid. And, believe it or not, in small-scale gold mining. It's in fluorescent lights and LCD screens like this one,' she replied, tapping her laptop. 'Light bulbs, TV screens and computer monitors are safe while they're in one piece. Break them and some mercury vapour will escape.'

'But people aren't dropping like flies.'

'No. I think we're safe, but it means some factories must keep a supply of it. That's where you could get it from.' Looking at the information scrolling down her screen, she said, 'It happens naturally in some ores and rocks. It's mined in a few different countries. And we used to put it in thermometers, batteries, felt, electrical switches, pesticides, some medicines and a few other things. There are some factories that take in this old stuff, remove the metal and recycle it.'

Troy nodded. 'Recycling centres sound good. I think I'd go to one of them to nick some. Let's check if any have reported mercury going missing.'

'I'll email the lot.'

'You said pesticides as well.'

Lexi scanned her database. 'Plant bulbs are dipped in mercuric chloride. It's a fungicide. But it doesn't just kill fungi. It says here that a hundred milligrams will damage major cells and a couple of grams will kill a seventy-kilogram major. It's sometimes used to preserve seed grain because it kills just about anything growing on the seeds.'

'But the poisoner in me wouldn't know which farm or garden centre to go to. I wouldn't know which one uses mercury. One of those recycling factories is a better bet.'

'Here's that medicine. Thiomersal is a mercury-based preservative in vaccines, but it's only used in tiny amounts – not dangerous levels – and it's being phased out. It's still in a 'flu vaccine.'

'So,' Troy said, 'our murderer might be a bad batch of vaccine.'

'Huh. I think there'd be more than four victims.'

Terabyte nodded. 'I'll keep monitoring in case any more turn up.'

'There's another medical one. Merbromin's an antiseptic. You put it on small cuts, but it's not used much any more. And there's always a few quack cures. You know. What people call traditional medicine – meaning it doesn't work. Cinnabar's natural – mercury sulphide mainly – and it's powdered and put into tonics for sore throats, cold sores and infections. It sounds stupid. Most of it goes straight through a human body – outer or major – without getting absorbed. So it doesn't poison anyone, but it doesn't do anything either – unless you're a major and you take loads of it or heat it up and breathe it in. Then you're dead.'

'Is that the lot?' Troy asked.

'Just about. There's a reference here that says the biggest sources nowadays are volcanoes, coal-burning power stations and waste incinerators – if they don't catch the mercury and recycle it.'

Troy smiled. 'I'm not convinced anyone would go to a volcano to get a murder weapon, but there's plenty of other places to choose from.'

# SCENE 4

*Monday 5th May, Late morning*

'I'm sorry,' Dr Miriam Thirteen said in a counselling room at the hospital. 'The lab report confirmed Miley died of mercury poisoning. There was too much damage to her body for us to save her.'

'But ... ' Miley's father found it hard to talk. 'Mercury. I don't ... How did it happen?'

'That's what we're here to find out,' Troy said softly.

'You're the police. Was she ... ?'

'We don't know. All we're investigating at this stage is what happened.'

'But … '

'There's nothing to suggest it was deliberate. It may be some horrible accident. We just don't know. But we'll find out, I promise.'

Miley's mother sobbed into a scrunched handkerchief.

Concentrating, Lexi was extracting every bit of information from Miley Quist's mobile phone.

Troy continued, 'Sometime in the last week or so, Miley tangled with mercury. It would really help if you could think back and tell me everything she did.'

Miley's dad shook his head hopelessly. 'She's been all over. I don't know what she's been up to. We've been … distracted.'

'Apart from school, where did she go? What did she like to do?'

'She was the best daughter you could … ' He put his head down and, for a few seconds, kept his thoughts to himself. Then, sniffing, he looked up again. 'A couple of music festivals, I think. Cycling, swimming, boxing, running, climbing. You name it, Miley does it. I mean … did it.'

'Which recently? Can you give me some idea?'

'She exhausts us, watching her go off here, there and everywhere. After school, sometimes before school, at weekends. Full of energy. She does her own thing. Always been an independent girl. We gave up trying to keep track. She was so … alive. Just like her grandma. Carefree.'

'Think back to when she came home from her last trip. Did she do anything or say anything about it?'

Her dad paused to think. 'I saw her rinsing out her swimming costume, so she must have been for a swim. She cleaned mud off her trainers as well.'

'Did you ask … ?'

Miley's father put his head in his hands and mumbled, 'Look. It's not easy. She was a free spirit. She took after my mother. Who's just passed on.' He looked up again, tears in his eyes. 'Miley loved her grandma. Spent a lot of time with her. But she needed a break, to mourn in her own way. Like I said, we've been thrown by it all. We're struggling to cope.' He sighed, trying to focus. 'When Miley got back, she said she felt better, she'd got it out of her system. She meant the grief. Then she was off out again. Other than that … ' He shrugged.

'I'm very sorry,' Troy said. 'I know it's a bad time to ask, but did she keep a diary – written or electronic?'

'A diary? No. Too busy doing. She couldn't sit still long enough to write anything.'

'Can I show you three pictures of other people? I want to find out if Miley knew them.'

Her father shrugged.

He shook his head when he saw the photos.

'They're called Richard Featherstone, Keaton Hathaway and Alyssa Bending. Do the names help?'

'No.'

Miley's mother could hardly see anything through her bloodshot eyes, but she spluttered, 'No.'

'Was she on any sort of medication?'

'She was as fit as a fiddle. Now look at her.'

Troy waited, allowing the upwelling of sorrow to subside a little, before he asked, 'Has she been vaccinated recently?'

'Not since she was a toddler.'

'As far as you know, has she eaten anything out of the ordinary? Perhaps something that no one else tried.'

'I don't know. She didn't say anything.'

'I don't want to pry, but can I ask what happened to her grandma?'

'Cancer.'

'Have any other relatives or friends been ill recently?'

'No, I don't think so.'

Lexi looked up and asked, 'Did she have a laptop or computer?'

'No. She did everything on her phone.'

With the mobile in her hand, Lexi said, 'Miley doesn't seem to have many contacts. Not a lot of friends.'

Her father nodded. 'That suited her. She didn't need or want them. She just got on with her own life.'

'Did she like school?' Troy asked.

'She wasn't bullied, if that's what you're thinking. Maybe because she was strong. Physically and mentally.'

'A lot of major girls rate their friends above their family,' Troy commented.

Miley's mother said, 'Her teachers told us she was a rare girl. Happy without friends. Her grandma was enough.'

'Did she have any enemies?'

Miley's mother went back into her protective shell.

Her father answered, 'No. Why should she? There was nothing to dislike. She was ... the best.'

# SCENE 5

*Monday 5th May, Night*

It was a long journey south to the industrial town of Pullover Creek. Stopping next to an enormous garden centre and plant nursery, Troy and Lexi got out of the driverless car and, for a few seconds, watched bats circling eerily near a streetlamp. In the nearest house, they spoke to Alyssa Bending's husband and two children. The smell from the lavish bouquets in their front room was almost overpowering. So sweet, it was almost sickly.

A toxicity report had concluded that the cause of Alyssa's death was mercury poisoning. Troy found out quickly that the Bending family did not know the other three victims, Alyssa wasn't taking any medicines, she didn't keep any form of diary and, as far as her husband knew, she had eaten only trustworthy food.

'Near the end,' Mr Bending said, 'I couldn't make much out. Her talking was mixed up.' He sighed and swallowed. 'She was trying to say something about the kids, me, love and fish, I think.'

'Fish?'

'It sounds strange to you, no doubt, but not to us. She worked in the aquatic part of the garden centre, selling pet fish among other things.' He put his arm around his daughter's shoulders. 'I think she said something about wishing we'd gone on more picnics together.' For a while, he was unable to control his tears.

Lexi interrupted. 'Do you know if the garden centre sterilizes their bulbs by dipping them in mercuric chloride?'

He wiped his cheeks and shook his head. 'I don't get involved in the technical side of things.'

'You work there as well?' asked Troy.

'In the gardening section.' He waved towards the bumper collection of bouquets. 'I do flower arrangements – and sell them.'

'Would Alyssa have had anything to do with pesticides?'

'No, definitely not. They don't mix with aquaria and fish.'

Troy nodded. 'Have you heard of any spillages or of any of your colleagues falling ill?'

'No.'

'How about you – or anyone else she knew? Has anyone else got the same symptoms?'

'No.'

'Did she get on all right with the garden centre, or were there any issues?'

'We've had arguments about noise and traffic, but we can't complain too much. It gives us a living.' Alyssa's husband broke down again. 'It gave us a living.'

Lexi examined Alyssa's laptop but found nothing relevant to her death or her recent movements. She looked at Mr Bending and asked, 'Can I see her mobile phone?'

Alyssa's husband sniffed and then replied, 'No. She lost it.'

'When?'

'She had a couple of days away last week. It was to do with work. She went off to the north coast to scout out sources of fish and supplies. Something she did now and again. When she fell ill, she told me she couldn't find her mobile. She said she must have lost it when she was away. Unless she was confused about that as well.'

# SCENE 6

Keaton Hathaway's flat in Pickling was decorated not with paintings, prints or photographs, but with crystals, fossils and rocks. A geological specimen seemed to rest on every flat surface. On the table, there was a clear plastic box with a rough mineral or mineral-like rock in each small compartment, like a collection of colourful eggs in individual nests. Each one had been lovingly labelled.

Lexi peered at the samples in turn. 'Jade, jet, gold, gypsum, feldspar, emerald, diamond, cinnabar.' She stopped reciting names and looked across at Troy.

'That's mercury sulphide.'

Ill at ease, Troy nodded as he wandered around.

Lexi moved towards a shelf and gasped at the selection of spiral fossils. 'He's got lots of ammonites. Never seen so many in one place. Fantastic. Shells as well.'

While Lexi admired Keaton's samples, Troy explored the small one-bedroom apartment. It took less than a minute. Then he said, 'He lived on his own – with a passion for geology.' He put on latex gloves, moved a couple of bones from a pile of notebooks on Keaton's desk and picked up the top one. Flicking through its pages, he soon realized that Keaton had recorded every find, every rock, every fossil.

Examining the windowsill, Lexi called out, 'There's a prehistoric fish here. Brilliant fossil.'

Troy held up the most recent diary. 'He was as methodical as you. Dates, locations, specimens, everything. A super-keen fossil hunter and amateur geologist. But why have the latest few pages been torn out?'

'Really?'

Troy sighed. 'Yes.'

'I'll bag it as evidence. I want to know who ripped them out. Fingerprints, DNA, anything.'

While outers and majors looked much the same, forensic science could easily distinguish the two human races. Their body chemistry was different. Outers bore no fingerprints, their DNA was distinctive, and their diet was based on insects. They also lacked the enzymes that made alcohol an intoxicating substance to majors.

'It wouldn't have been Keaton himself,' Troy said. 'Looks like he's obsessive about keeping records. If he made a mistake, he'd cross it out, not remove it. Then he'd have a record of the mistake as well.'

'I'll request a full forensic team. They can hunt for the missing pages – as well as any trace evidence. And I'll get them to scan all his notebooks into a database.' Lexi stood beside her partner to examine the journal.

Troy tilted it towards her. 'The last ten days have gone.'

'It might have told us when and where he was poisoned – and where the mercury came from.'

Muted, Troy shrugged.

'Don't tell me it's coincidence, because I don't believe it.' Lexi glanced at him and added, 'Are you okay?'

'Yes,' he replied.

'Sure?'

He took a deep breath. 'If you must know, Pickling's not my favourite place.'

'You must have been here before.'

'No,' he almost snapped.

'So, how do you know you don't like it?'

'I just don't. Let's leave it at that.'

# SCENE 7

Richard Featherstone's bedroom in Hoops was a mess, like a grotesque, bloodied murder scene. His wife had barely touched the place where he had died. If she had slept at all since his death, she must have laid down somewhere else. Lexi looked at the mercury thermometer on a shelf. It was unbroken. It could not be the source of the mercury that had poisoned him.

Downstairs, Mrs Featherstone looked out of the window as the sun slowly submerged below the horizon. 'We were ... okay, you know. At the stage where the passion had gone out of it – worn down by time, children and other demands. You know. Maybe you don't. You're young. Anyway, that's what happens. We were busy. Other things gobbled up our time. Less time for each other. We were fine, though. Still cared for each other very much. Plenty of respect. No doubt about that.'

She seemed jittery to Troy. He guessed that the words spilling from her were not so much information for a detective as an attempt to convince herself that she'd shared a loving relationship with Richard. But he noticed that she avoided talking about love.

'I thought he'd got a hangover, you know. That's all. I wasn't even sympathetic. He'd been out with mates for a drink and he'd had too much. What was I supposed to think?' She groaned. 'Bad mistake. I should've called a doctor when he talked about his hands and feet being numb.'

'I don't think it would've made any difference,' Troy said gently. 'By that time, he was almost certainly beyond medical help.' He gazed at her kindly, knowing that his questions would cause her further pain. 'Was he often out doing his own thing?'

'Yes. But he always came back to me. A married

couple need their separate interests after a while, don't you think?'

'Do you know the things he did in the last week or so?'

'Some.' She sighed. 'I should've asked more. I regret that. He went fishing one day. On his own. Golf with friends, I think. That's at Hoops Golf Course. I don't know where he went fishing. He had tickets for a football match, I think. Or something like that. He trotted off to his friends' houses for drinks – and to one of the pubs in town. I don't go. A glass of wine and you'd have to hold me up. Goes straight to my head, you know. Richard, well, he could knock back quite a bit. Not like an outer, though. He got woozy and he'd have a sore head in the morning. Sometimes, he'd be sick.' She shook her head sadly at her husband's foolishness. 'Now, I wonder if he was getting his excitement that way instead of getting it with me.'

'Was he on any sort of medication, or was he vaccinated recently?'

'He took hangover cures. That's all. Only they don't cure anything, do they? Not drinking alcohol in the first place is the only proper cure.'

Troy took a gulp of water. 'You said you'd looked at his phone.'

'Yes. Funny, that. Nothing on it at all. He'd reset it. No stored phone numbers or anything else. I don't know why. My guess is that he'd tried to call me. You know, just before he got really bad and passed out. Maybe he hit the wrong button. That's almost certainly it, don't you think?'

Clearly she was hoping there was nothing sinister or secretive in Richard's actions, so he replied, 'Confusion's one of the symptoms – along with poor memory and tremors – so, yes, you're probably right.' He showed her the images of the other three patients and told her their names. 'Do you know any of them? Or do you think Richard would've known them?'

'I certainly don't. As for Richard … ' She shrugged. 'I wouldn't know. I should've asked after his friends more. I shouldn't have let the gulf grow wider and wider.'

'It's not your fault. Being close takes two people.' Troy's attention seemed to stray but, a moment later, he was fully focused on the interview. 'I don't suppose you asked much about the food he'd been eating or any strange drinks he'd tried?'

'No. We should've shared more, like it used to be when we were young.'

Outside, the sun ducked behind a building and was gone.

'Do you know if any of his friends have gone down with something similar?'

'No, I don't. If only I'd taken the trouble to ... ' The sentence faded to nothing.

'What did he do by way of work?'

'He was always artistic. He could paint, model wood, almost anything. Really good with his hands. Creative. He used to make hats. Now, he makes furniture.'

'Hats?' Lexi queried.

Richard's wife smiled sorrowfully. 'Yes, hats. Someone's got to do it. Richard switched to furniture about a year ago.'

'Was he well? Did the hat job make him sick?' said Lexi.

'No. Why?'

'I bet you've heard the phrase: mad as a hatter,' Lexi replied. 'Rabbits' or hares' fur was made into felt and mercuric nitrate was used to smooth it down. A slow reaction in the felt gave off mercury vapour. It made hatters tetchy and mixed up. Basically, a bit mad.'

'No. Nothing like that,' his wife replied. 'Besides, it was a long time ago. I wish I'd asked him more about his jobs. You do at first but then ... your mind's on other things, you know, and you get tired of hearing the same old story every day.'

'Did he keep a diary or jot notes on a computer?' Troy asked.

'No. Not when there's golf to play. Nothing else got much of a look in.' She sighed once more. 'If only I'd developed an interest in golf. Things might have been different.'

# SCENE 8

*Wednesday 7th May, Morning*

The beginnings of a spreadsheet decorated the large screen in the forensic department of Shepford Crime Central. Lexi sipped beer and ate cricket pâté on banana worm bread as she entered data methodically.

'Shepford in the middle of the country, Pullover Creek and Hoops down south, and Pickling up north. Not even close on an atlas. A school student, a seller of pet fish, a furniture maker and a fossil hunter. Pick a common factor out of that lot, if you can. By the way, Keaton's real job was in his local insect farm. Yummy.'

'An insect farm?' As part of his breakfast, Troy swallowed a chunk of black pudding.

'You don't have to be an outer to make outer food. But he wasn't the most dedicated worker. He cracked open more rocks than water beetles. More interested in hunting fossils than producing meat.' She paused, thinking. 'There's a sort of common thread between two of them. One deleted everything from his phone and another lost hers. Richard Featherstone and Alyssa Bending.'

'That link's hanging by a thread,' Troy replied with a grin. 'Way south of solid. Both could have been an accident.'

'Yeah. But it's about all we've got. Except that all four were healthy before they died. Swimming, cycling, climbing, chasing fish around the country, golf, smashing rocks.'

'What did you get from Keaton Hathaway's latest notebook?'

'I went through it last night. No fingerprints – which means a careful major ripped the pages out with gloves on, or it was an outer. But there was a hair. Human, silver colour. Short. A bit like mine. Before you ask, no, I'm sure it's not contamination. It's not mine.'

'Good find. I hope you're giving it some welly.'

'I would, but you keep dragging me off to the four corners of the country. I've given it to the specialists to analyse the DNA in the root. Waiting for results. They'll tell us for sure it's not mine.'

'Did the forensic team find anything else in his flat?'

'Lots, but what's relevant and what's nothing to do with it? No mercury except for the tiny amounts in his rock samples. And they didn't find the torn-out pages.'

'We're at a crossroads,' said Troy. 'But instead of three ways to go we've got hundreds.' He shrugged. 'I don't want to follow up Richard Featherstone first because the woman who knew him best hardly knows anything. Married, but barely in touch with each other. She's not going to help much. I think Alyssa's a better way forward. I'm going to contact the garden centre where she worked.'

It didn't take him long to set up a video call to the manager of Pullover Creek Garden Centre and Plant Nursery. After introducing himself and his investigation, Troy said, 'Alyssa Bending. She worked in your aquatic centre.'

The manager nodded. 'Yes. I was very upset to hear the news. We all were. It's bad enough for us here in the garden centre. It must be awful for her family.'

'Do you use mercuric nitrate for sterilizing bulbs?'

On-screen, she looked surprised for an instant. 'Not for ages. No. It's harmful.'

'Do you still have old stock?' Troy asked.

'I'd be very surprised. But I'll check and let you know if we do. What's this got to do with Alyssa?'

'I heard you sent her on various trips to fish suppliers.'

'Yes. It was part of her job description. She got to go all over the place. She took advantage, mind.'

'Oh?'

'I'm not complaining. I'd have done the same. If it was somewhere nice or the weather was really good, she'd turn a half-day outing into a day. A day's worth of work got turned into two days.' The manager smiled. 'She tacked on mini-holidays.'

'When was her last trip, where did she go and how long did she take?'

The manager checked out a monitor on her desk. 'Yes. She went to a fish breeder in Tight End on Friday the twenty-fifth of April. I put aside a day for it, but she didn't come back to work on the Saturday. I don't know what she did afterwards. It might have been because it was a lovely weekend up on the north coast. Like summer. Warm and sunny.'

'Thanks,' Troy replied. 'That's helpful.' He

terminated the call and turned to his partner. 'Good lead. Fancy a trip to Tight End?'

'A few hours alone with you in a car? To the fifth corner of the country? Sounds great.'

He ignored Lexi's jokey sarcasm. 'I knew you'd jump at the chance. Plenty of opportunity for you to meditate.'

Like most majors, Troy had just rested his body with a long period of overnight sleep. Outers like Lexi refreshed themselves with short periods of meditation. Several times each day, she would turn off for fifteen minutes. The distances that they were travelling in this case were ideal for her regular relaxation.

Lexi clicked the keypad of her computer. 'There's a recycling factory there. It deals with batteries and that sort of thing. Worth a visit.' She hesitated before adding, 'By the way, no recycling centres have got back to me about thefts or break-ins. No mercury reported missing recently.' Browsing more tourism information, she said, 'Thinking about Richard Featherstone, there's a golf course somewhere near Tight End as well.'

'There's a golf course somewhere near everywhere.'

'Yeah. True. There's a sports centre down the road

towards Loose End. No swimming pool, but it's got a gym, climbing centre, running track and a velodrome for cycling. That might have attracted Miley Quist.'

'What about Keaton Hathaway?'

'Last night I checked every single scan of his notebooks – and copied the lot into our life-loggers. There's no mention of Loose End or Tight End.'

'Maybe there was on the bits that got torn out. Let's go take a look.'

# SCENE 9

*Wednesday 7th May, Afternoon*

It was difficult to imagine that, ten days ago, Tight End had enjoyed a summery weekend. As Troy and Lexi emerged from their car, a fierce wind blew rain almost horizontally across the town. The young detectives leaned into the gale and dashed to the fish breeding centre. They slammed the door, shutting out the raging storm. Inside, the reception was calm and warm. An oasis. Brightly coloured tropical fish flashed inside rows of tanks. Air bubbling through the water made a soothing gurgle and the lights of the aquaria shimmered attractively.

Lexi and Troy shook the raindrops from their coats while they waited to see a supervisor. Fascinated by the hypnotic movement of the fish, Lexi said, 'I've always fancied being a scuba diver. Swimming with fish, especially sharks. They're powerful, sleek and charismatic.'

The supervisor entered the reception and, overhearing her, said with a smile, 'We don't keep them, I'm afraid. We only supply fish that are quite a bit smaller.'

Once he had introduced himself, he sat down with two fish tanks behind him at shoulder-height. The detectives took seats opposite him. Troy angled for answers and Lexi gazed at fish.

Showing an image of Alyssa Bending on his lifelogger, Troy said, 'Have you had a visit from her recently?'

'From the rather nicely named Pullover Creek Garden Centre, as I recall.'

'When was she here?'

The supervisor consulted his small laptop. 'Friday the twenty-fifth. April, that is.'

'Did she seem okay to you? I mean, she didn't look ill or anything?'

'Quite the opposite. She looked very happy.'

'And she didn't have any accidents while she was here?'

'No. Nothing like that.'

'Did she say where she was going next?'

The supervisor took a breath as he thought about it. 'I don't think so. I didn't ask. It was all very business-like.'

'Do you use mercury-containing pesticides?'

Shocked at the suggestion, he said, 'Absolutely not. Read the small print on almost any pesticide. *Harmful to aquatic organisms. Keep away from fish. Causes long-term damage to aquatic environments.* That sort of thing. So, no, we don't allow any in the building at all. On pain of death.' He hesitated for an instant. 'That's a joke, by the way.'

Showing the photographs of the other three victims, Troy asked, 'Have any of these people ever dropped in?' He recited their names.

'No.'

'Did you do a deal with Alyssa?'

'She was impressed with our quality. Anyone would be. She ordered some chevron tang, mandarin fish and quite a few tetras. With options for others later.'

'And that was it? Nothing unusual to tell me?'

'No. Oh, you asked about where she was going. I left her here in reception but I remember she went up to the desk ... ' He turned and called out to the receptionist, 'That rep from Pullover Creek Garden Centre. Did I hear her ask you for directions?'

'Erm. I believe she did, yes.'

'Where to?' Troy asked.

'It was … er … a restaurant.'

'Any particular one?'

The receptionist paused, his fingers fiddling with a small gold badge on his lapel. 'I think it was the Doom Merchant. That's where most people go around here.'

'Weird name,' Troy said with a frown.

The supervisor smiled wryly. 'Someone's idea of wit. It stands for Dining Outers Or Majors.'

Troy faced Lexi and said, 'Fancy a bite to eat?'

The Doom Merchant was huge. It had one large dining area and several side rooms for small groups. On each table were two menus. One was labelled *Major Feasts* and it was a list of meals based on animal protein, designed for majors. The other was called *Ins and Outs*, offering a varied insect diet for outers.

Troy and Lexi ordered their separate meals before showing the waiter a photograph of Alyssa Bending. He glanced at the image, shrugged helplessly and waved an arm vaguely around his busy restaurant.

'There are probably a few in right now who look quite like her.'

'If she booked in advance ... '

Impatiently, the waiter interrupted. 'We don't take bookings. It's first come, first served.'

Wind and rain battered the nearest window, as if trying to get through to the two detectives.

While she waited for her fried locusts with chilli and lime, Lexi used her life-logger to circulate Alyssa's name and image to all hotels in the area. 'She must have stayed somewhere overnight,' she said to her partner.

Troy nodded. 'Worth a try, but she could have gone a long way before bedtime.'

'We'll see.' Lexi looked at him and said, 'In case you're wondering, no one online is moaning about food poisoning or feeling ill after visiting the Doom Merchant. Hey presto, no mercury in the meals.'

'That's comforting.'

Lexi examined her life-logger again and said, 'Switch to Pickling mode. I've just got the results on the hair from Keaton Hathaway's journal. The DNA wasn't mine. Don't know whose it is. The profile wasn't in any database. But here's the good news. I asked the specialists to give me the best picture they could from analysing the DNA. First, it's a man's –

almost certainly. Definitely an outer, probably brown eyes. He might be taller than average, but that's little better than a guess. Is that enough welly for you?'

Troy smiled. 'Yeah. Shiveringly good.'

Lexi let her life-logger hang on her waist again. Keeping her voice just above the hubbub in the restaurant, she said, 'I've been meaning to ask. What have you got against Pickling?'

At once, a cloud came over Troy.

He was saved from finding an immediate answer by the waiter, who returned with a grey squirrel pie for a major and fried locusts for an outer.

After he'd gone and they'd both begun their separate meals, Troy said, 'I don't talk about this. I've never told anyone. But you're ... different.' He studied his fork for a moment, before finding the courage to continue. 'Pickling's got a prison. That's where my dad is.'

'You mean he's a guard? Or ... ' She stopped as she looked into his sombre face.

'No, he's not a guard.'

'Oh,' Lexi gasped. 'What happened?'

'It's a long story.' For Troy, the other diners had dissolved. It was just him, his memories and the matter-of-fact outer girl who had become a friend as well as a work partner. 'You'd probably look it up in police files if I didn't tell you, so … It started with Mum. Like my dad, she was a police officer. She was off-duty one day when she saw two thugs – lads with guns – go for a much older man. Thinking it was a mugging – as anyone would – she stepped in, protecting the man on his own. It was an impulse thing.' Troy gazed down at his plateful of pie, soaked in brown sauce. 'She saved him. She took the bullets herself.'

As an outer, Lexi didn't have parents, but she knew that they meant a great deal to majors. She said nothing. Instead, she reached out and touched his arm.

After a few seconds, Troy looked up again. 'The funny thing was who the older man was. The godfather of a gang. Blackmail, drug dealing, armed robbery, people trafficking, the lot. The lads who attacked him were two of his victims.' He sighed and wiped his eyes. 'The gang was very grateful. The boss "compensated" Dad. Made sure he was "comfortable". I was too young to know what was going on. I just knew I didn't have a mother any more. I like to think Dad refused the money at first, but … I don't know. He started getting all sorts of favours. His next cases got solved when witnesses came forward. I guess, being on the inside, the gang knew who was up to what and delivered the culprits to Dad. Suddenly he was north of successful and had wall-to-wall cash.' Troy shook his head. 'The next step was the worst. The boss paid him to look the other way while they were doing jobs. To cut the story short, a detective got whiff of a nasty smell and Dad was done for corruption.'

'The law comes down heavily when it's a police officer who's been turned.'

'Yes.'

'I'm sorry.'

'Yeah.'

'You said you'd never been to Pickling. I know prison visits aren't exactly encouraged, but haven't you been to see him?'

'No.' Troy looked up at the ceiling before adding, 'Two muggers robbed me of a mother but you don't expect your own dad to rob you of a father.'

The storm had blown itself out. It ceased to hammer on the window.

Lexi gazed sadly at her partner. Deciding that he'd had enough, she said, 'I don't know about squirrel pie, but locusts aren't improved by being cold.'

Feeling oddly lighter in mood, Troy tucked into his tepid pie. At the same time, he applied his mind to the investigation. It was a sure way of burying more painful thoughts. Between mouthfuls, he said, 'That connection you made – two mobiles, one lost and the other reset. You might have a point. If you think of mobiles as places to put information, Richard's and Alyssa's have both gone. It's a pity phone records aren't backed up to some great big remote database. Anyway, Keaton wrote information down in a notebook. His latest has gone. A brown-eyed, silver-haired male outer probably ripped it out. Miley never stored it in her phone or wrote it down in the first place.' He shrugged. 'Missing information. I suppose it's more a case of things turning out the same than a real connection. So … '

'We carry on looking.'

'Exactly. And hope we recognize the link when it's staring us in the face.'

'We'll see.'

# SCENE 10

*Wednesday 7th May, Late afternoon*

The chief scientist of Tight End Recycling Facility – an outer called Caroline Seventeen – pointed to a metallic contraption, about the same height as Troy, and said proudly, 'This is state-of-the-art. As far as I'm aware, it's the best available technology in the country for removing and capturing mercury. No other processor comes close. It makes recycling easy.'

The grey box, about a metre wide and another metre deep, had several digital monitors and control buttons on the front. A large silvery chimney was attached to the top. The shiny vent rose vertically and disappeared into the roof of the building.

'It's a retort, basically,' Caroline explained. 'A hi-tech incinerator. It burns any household item containing mercury – thermometers, fluorescent lamps, LCD screens and flat-screen TVs are the main ones – and filters organic gases from the waste stream. A highly efficient condenser and cold trap captures the mercury. Over ninety-nine per cent of it.'

'And then what happens to it?' Troy asked.

'The recovered metal's completely sealed in a safe receiver. We sell it to companies that need it to make new products.'

'What's your safety record like? Any accidental release of mercury in the last week or two?'

'Our record's perfect,' she claimed proudly. 'It has to be. The whole process happens under a slight vacuum so, if there's any leak, air goes in and contaminated air doesn't come out. We monitor performance at all stages, twenty-four seven. We keep all the data if you want to see it.'

Lexi said, 'I get all that. It's impressive, but it can't be as clean and easy as you make out. If the lamps and screens aren't broken, perhaps it's all smooth. But what if someone's getting rid of a broken thermometer or a cracked computer screen? The mercury's already leaking.'

At once, Caroline realized that Lexi was a forensic scientist. She launched into a lecture. 'As long as the integrity of the item isn't compromised, recycling's straightforward, as you suggest. We've got different procedures in place to deal with samples that aren't intact. First, the owner places the damaged device in one of our recycling containers and then we look after it from that point. All my workers are fully trained, have the highest level safety equipment, and they're monitored for signs of mercury contamination. We've got an outstanding health and safety record, fully approved by the relevant environmental agency and complying with all regulations for processing hazardous waste.'

Troy smiled. Clearly she had delivered exactly the same message many times to clients, visitors and the environmental authorities.

'Who's he, over there?' Lexi asked, pointing to a worker in a fluorescent yellow jacket. The man was taller than Lexi but he had the same short hair, somewhere between silver and blonde.

'Jon Drago Five,' Caroline replied. 'In charge of the distribution of recovered mercury.'

'Perhaps he could join us,' Troy suggested.

The chief scientist called over the brown-eyed outer.

'You might be able to help us,' Troy said. 'I was about to ask where the mercury goes from here.'

'We have a safe collection point at that end of the building,' Jon answered, waving to the right. 'That's my domain. A fleet of secure vans carry sealed, impact-proof containers to their destinations. That's when it's out of our hands and under the control of a manufacturer.'

'Do you go out on deliveries?'

He shook his head.

Caroline added, 'You've only gone out on a run if you've needed to discuss something with the business it's going to.'

'That's true,' Jon agreed.

'Do you keep a log? I guess you must do,' said Troy.

'The regulations are clear. We have to account for every gram – where it goes and when.'

'Have you been to – or through – Pickling in the last couple of weeks? If you're not sure, consult the log.'

'I don't need to,' Jon replied. 'I know we haven't made any deliveries there for a while.'

'Is there any point in the process where mercury

could go missing and you wouldn't know about it?' Troy asked.

Caroline and Jon exchanged a glance. 'Look,' Caroline said. 'I'm well aware of our responsibility to keep mercury out of the environment. I'm well aware of what can happen if someone gets sloppy, especially if it leaks into water and gets into the fish and water-borne creatures that majors eat. There was a case in Japan – a coastal fishing town. A factory dumped methylmercury – extremely poisonous – in the sea. Children and unborn babies are particularly sensitive to it. It was tragic. Hundreds died. People who ate the local seafood – and the ones who ate meat from animals fed on the local fish – lost control of their bodies. So did their pets and feeding birds. That's the effect of methylmercury on the brain. Half of them died and major women gave birth to horribly deformed children. It's said – I don't know how true it is – that some babies were born without brains. So, yes, everyone at TERF takes their duties very seriously.'

Jon said, 'Once we hand a consignment over to the end client, though, it's their responsibility, not ours.'

'But,' Caroline added quickly, 'I vet my entire workforce *and* the destination businesses. They've got all the necessary licences. I make sure we don't have any rogues at any point in the chain.'

'So, you don't mind giving me a list of employees and clients?'

'I'll send it to your life-logger within twenty-four hours.'

'Thanks,' Troy said. 'One final thing.' He lifted up his life-logger and showed the victims' pictures. 'Do either of you know these people? Richard Featherstone, Miley Quist, Alyssa Bending and Keaton Hathaway.'

The two outers both shook their heads.

Looking into Jon Drago Five's face, Troy said, 'Sure?'

He turned his head away, covered his mouth with his hand and coughed loudly. Then he replied, 'Yes, I'm sure.'

Loose End was smaller and sleepier than its sibling town. Built beside a river, the quaint village seemed to be a place where nothing really happened. Behind it, a range of hills rose up impressively, almost vertically, dwarfing the village. Once popular with climbers, the rock face was riddled with caverns. It was topped by Loose End Edge. Further along, waterfalls plunged over the peaks and splashed into pools and rivers below.

Lexi looked up at Loose End Edge and said, 'If I lived around here, I'd be hang-gliding from there. Fantastic – jumping off and just drifting in the sky. I've always fancied being an instructor. Nice job.'

Distracted, Troy watched a grey squirrel running drunkenly along the branch of a roadside tree, until he lost sight of it in the foliage.

Loose End Sports lay between the village and its bigger partner, Tight End. Its facilities attracted clients from both places – and from further afield. Just inside the main entrance to the gym, indoor climbing centre, running track and velodrome, Troy spoke to a formidable-looking receptionist. She looked at the photo on Troy's life-logger carefully and then shook her head. 'I don't forget faces. Not a single one. As I don't know hers, she's certainly not been here while I've been on duty. Miley Quist is her name, you say.' She scrolled down a list of members on her monitor. 'Just as I thought. Not a member. Sorry. I can't help you.'

'As your memory for faces is so good, what about these three?' Troy said, showing the other victims.

'No. Definitely not.'

'That's that, then,' Lexi murmured.

'Thanks,' Troy said to the receptionist.

Hesitating before they left the sports centre, Lexi

told her partner, 'And the bad news just keeps rolling in. The local hotels, bed and breakfast places and that sort of thing have no record of an overnight stay by anyone called Alyssa Bending and no one recognized her face.'

'Let's go back to headquarters,' Troy suggested. 'It'll be late before we get there.'

Lexi shrugged. 'Doesn't bother me. I'll meditate on the way. You could try to get some sleep.'

'It's too early. Anyway, my brain's full of the case, back at that crossroads, working out what to do next.'

'Huh. You should learn to turn off and then back on again. It works wonders.'

After her second bout of meditation in the fast-moving car, Lexi's mind was particularly sharp. She took her life-logger in her hands and typed madly.

'What's up?' Troy asked.

'That hair at Keaton Hathaway's place. I think there's something else I can do with it. Not one of the routine tests. Something more ... experimental. I'm sure I heard about a new method. Yes. Here it is. 'Determining where people live by measuring the ratios of oxygen and hydrogen isotopes in their tissues.' And, yes, it includes hair.'

'How does that work? Or won't my feeble major

brain understand it even after you've explained it?'

'Well, I'll do my best to get it through to you despite your deficiencies.' She speed-read the article she'd found and then cleared her throat. 'When you live somewhere, your body absorbs chemicals from the water and food. You are what you eat. The ratio of isotopes oxygen-sixteen and oxygen-eighteen are different in different places. Same with hydrogen and deuterium. The plants, insects and farm animals we eat absorb the same pattern of isotopes so, as long as you eat mainly local food and drink local water, you get the same ratios in your body. In other words, the chemicals provide a tell-tale signature in your tissues.'

'There's a way of measuring these isotopes, then?'

'Mass spectrometry.'

'If you did it on my hair and yours, could you tell that you live in one Shepford zone and I live in another?'

'No chance. We're too close. Our water would come from the same source. But it'd easily tell different countries apart and different regions of the same country. It'd be good to know which region that male outer came from, wouldn't it?'

'Sure would. But what if he travels around a lot or only drinks bottled water?'

'That would be the end of that. It's got to be someone who eats quite a bit of local food and drinks loads of local water – from a tap. Then I just compare the two isotope ratios in the hair with a database of the same ratios from different parts of the country – and overseas. If there's a match, hey presto, we know the region where he eats and drinks.'

'Nice idea. Shiveringly good idea. What's stopping you from cracking on with it?'

Lexi frowned and glanced theatrically round the inside of the automatic car. 'It's not equipped with a mass spectrometer and I forgot to bring the hair sample.'

Troy rolled his eyes. 'I meant, calling the forensic department and getting them on the job.'

'It's not a recognized method. I'm going to have to work out how best to do it with some specialists when we get back. And I'm thinking about trying another test as well.'

Troy nodded. 'Something useful for you to do while I'm tucked up in bed.'

'What's your busy brain come up with so far?'

'We're still on the nursery slopes of this investigation. I want to ask Richard Featherstone's mates where he was on the weekend of the twenty-sixth and twenty-seventh of April. We need to check out Jon Drago Five – just in case. And I'd like to visit the insect farm where Keaton Hathaway worked.'

Lexi licked her lips. 'Now you're talking.'

# SCENE 11

*Wednesday 7th May, Night*

'Hi, Gran. It's me.'

'Late again,' Troy's grandma replied. It wasn't a criticism, just a fact.

'Sorry.'

'Your dad was the same. Working all hours of the night and day.' She stopped herself and glanced at Troy.

'It's okay,' he said. 'I ... er ... talked about him today – and about Mum. To Lexi. It felt right.'

'Lexi, eh?'

'Yes.'

'Still working with the same girl, then?'

'Yes. Still getting on well.'

Grandma frowned. 'It's working with an outer that keeps you away from home. That's what I think anyway. They work around the clock so you think you've got to follow suit. But you don't. You can't. You need your sleep.'

'Lexi ribs me about it, but she knows. It's not her fault I'm late, Gran. It's the case. We've just got back from Loose End.'

'Oh. There's something I've got to tell you, honey. Watch yourself by the back door.'

'Why?'

'The drain from the kitchen sink got blocked. When I was clearing it, a rat came up out of the sewer. I called someone.'

'And they put poison down?'

'Yes. Nasty stuff. We mustn't touch it.'

'Okay.'

'So, where's Loose End?'

'Way up on the north coast. A few hours away.'

'Couldn't they get some local people to deal with it?' She smiled at him and added, 'I know you're the best and all that, but surely there's someone up north who can do the job.'

'It's a weird case, Gran. Some of it's here in

Shepford. The rest is anywhere from Hoops – near the south coast – to Loose End. I'll be travelling a lot.'

'Oh. Well, it's good to get around. Nice to see somewhere different. Like going on holiday.'

Troy grinned. 'It doesn't feel like a holiday.'

Grandma didn't ask for any details. Over the years, she'd had enough of hearing about police work. She'd had enough of tragedies. She heaved herself out of her armchair. 'Never mind. Come into the kitchen. There's something for you in the oven.'

Remembering how Lexi had reacted to the idea of visiting an insect farm, Troy licked his lips. 'Now you're talking.'

# SCENE 12

Lexi welcomed her partner back to work with a grimace. 'There's a hitch with the isotope analysis.'

'But you're a forensic genius. I thought you'd tell me where the man with the hair lived as soon as I walked through the door.'

'It's not straightforward. But I've briefed the experts and they've got the hair. They'll do it as soon as they can. There's another issue with it, though.'

'What's that?'

'The legal people are studying it. They reckon the result might not be presentable in court because it's not a recognized forensic test. It's not been validated for use in law.'

'That fits,' Troy said with a sigh. 'But the result will still be useful to us.'

'Yeah. That's why I told them to go ahead anyway.'

Troy gazed at her face for a moment and said, 'Being the perceptive one, I think you're bursting to tell me more. You've given me the bad news first and now you're going to cheer me up with something fantastic.'

'Huh. Not fantastic, but interesting.'

'What is it?'

'It's the same hair.'

'It's amazing what forensics can get from one tiny strand.'

'Yeah. I checked it for mercury concentration and did some comparisons. My hair contains four parts per million of mercury. Almost nothing. I'm not dying of mercury poisoning. Keaton Hathaway's hair is 705 parts per million – or ppm as us scientists call it. That's extreme. No wonder the mercury killed him. I measured the hair in his diary at 165 ppm of mercury.'

'An in-between figure.'

'So, you're not a complete dud at maths. Yes. It's an outer who's been around mercury quite a lot.'

Troy nodded. 'Interesting.'

'Yeah. That's what I said.'

'Nice work.'

'If we're looking at murder – if it was deliberate – I still don't know why the bad guy opted for mercury, though. It's a strange choice.' Lexi hesitated, thinking, before she carried on. 'I mean, everything's a poison. It's not so much about what gets into your body. It's more about how much gets in. We all die if we drink too much water or swallow enough salt. No matter what it is, if it's more than your body can cope with, you're poisoned. So, if you were going to poison someone, there are better ways of doing it. Much easier than mercury. Like poisons that kill in such tiny amounts that they don't leave a trace.'

'You're on fire today.'

'I hope not.'

'Me, I'm struggling with motive,' Troy admitted. 'Why those four people?'

'Maybe this just adds up to an accident – a mini-version of the Japanese mercury pollution story that Caroline Seventeen told us about.'

'And it killed people in Shepford, Pickling, Pullover Creek and Hoops?'

'Yeah. Okay. We're still looking for the fatal connection.'

'Talking of Hoops ... '

Lexi nodded. 'A round of golf with Richard Featherstone's friends?'

'Exactly.' Troy paused before adding, 'And talking of people who work at Tight End Recycling Facility ...'

'We need to run that check on Jon Drago Five.'

'Come on. We can start it on the way.'

# SCENE 13

---

*Thursday 8th May, Late morning*

Speeding southward in the car, Troy said, 'I wish we'd got a DNA sample from Jon Drago Five when we were at TERF – to see if it matches the hair.'

'We don't have a reason to make him a suspect,' Lexi replied. 'Matching a vague description isn't enough. Hundreds of other male outers would do that.'

'I know. But he works with mercury.'

'Still not a good enough excuse to grab his DNA.'

All police officers wore life-loggers to record everything they did and said. The recordings were used to make sure that every investigation had been carried out correctly. The devices also prevented most attacks on police officers, because the crooks knew that their actions would be captured on video and transmitted to the nearest police computer.

'But if we turn up anything shifty about him … ' Troy left the sentence hanging in mid-air.

'We'll see. But remember Caroline Seventeen said she'd vetted him.'

'We've got bigger and better databases. And you're more thorough.'

Lexi laughed. 'Yeah. More methodical.'

Troy said, 'Caroline probably vetted him for scientific competence and honesty. We're vetting him for poisoning. Has he got any friends – or, more importantly, enemies – who've been ill? Does he have a police record? Does he run a black market in mercury? Do all TERF's checks and balances add up, or has someone fiddled the figures?'

'No matter how thorough and methodical I am, I don't think I'm going to get all the answers in a car that's going in the exact opposite direction from where he lives,' Lexi replied. 'I'll get onto Tight End Crime Central and see if they can spare us a local to dig around.'

'That figures.'

'We've got a list of TERF's workers and clients as well. Loads of leads in there.'

'That's one thing we're not short of. Things to investigate.'

They spent the rest of the journey researching the people and organizations on Caroline Seventeen's list of contacts. That included Jon Drago Five.

'Here's something,' Lexi said. 'Well, not very much, but a company called Switcher – they make electronic switches – buys some of TERF's mercury and they're based in Pickling. Not far from Keaton Hathaway.'

Troy nodded. 'Onto the spreadsheet with them.' He took a breath and then said, 'Jon Drago Five doesn't work at weekends. I don't know where he was on the twenty-sixth and twenty-seventh of last month.'

'His numbers add up, though,' Lexi replied. 'I've been through TERF's records. The amount of mercury they've reclaimed over the years is the same as the amount they've sold plus the stock they say they're holding right now.'

'So, if someone's hijacking a bit, they're cooking the books as well.'

'Yeah. It'd be somebody with access to the company's computer and all its logs. Or maybe

they've got less mercury on site than they think –
because some's been nicked.'

After a few more minutes, Lexi exclaimed, 'Hey.
Listen to this.' Her life-logger piped rock music into
the car and, for a while, her head nodded in rhythm.
'Mmm. Not bad.'

'What is it?' Troy asked.

'A group called Mercury Splash.'

'Choosing a name like that doesn't make them
guilty of poisoning.'

'The drummer's good, though, isn't he?'

Suspicious, Troy said, 'What are you getting at?'

'I know what Jon Drago Five does at weekends.
He packs up his drum kit and tours with Mercury
Splash.'

'Really?'

'Yes.'

'Unusual for an outer to play music.'

'Some say the drums aren't a musical instrument.
Anyway, even outers can keep time. The rest of the
group are majors.'

'So, where have Mercury Splash been gigging for
the last few weekends?'

'Thought you'd never ask. Quite a few places. I've
downloaded a list. The ones we're interested in are
Pickling and Shepford.'

Troy nodded. 'Yesterday, Jon Five told us he hadn't been to Pickling for a while.'

'That's right. But, to be fair, he was talking about not making any deliveries there.'

'Still, it's a bit strange he didn't mention it.'

'Musicians!' Lexi muttered. 'They never know what town they're in when they're on tour.'

Troy laughed. 'Playing a gig or two each weekend isn't what I'd call a tour. Anyway, you've got a definite link to Pickling and Shepford. That's a possible link to Keaton Hathaway and Miley Quist. And Miley's dad said she went to a music festival. But … ' He hesitated and shook his head. 'Would you call yourself Mercury Splash if you were about to kill people with mercury?'

'Maybe the name of the group came first. Then changing it would look even more suspicious.' She checked her life-logger again. 'They played Shepford Music Festival a couple of weekends back.'

'What about the Pickling gig? Did your forensic team find a ticket for it at Keaton Hathaway's place?'

'No. Not one of the items they logged.'

Troy called Alyssa Bending's husband and asked if Alyssa had been to see a group called Mercury Splash. Mr Bending couldn't be sure, but he doubted it. The band was more likely to appeal to his children than to his wife.

Troy ended the call and sighed. 'This connection is looking south of certain, but I'll ask Richard Featherstone's mates if he's the sort to go and see Mercury Splash.'

'Good idea.'

What was left of the morning was clear and bright. From the large window of the clubhouse at Hoops Golf Course, Troy could just see the south coast. The eyesight of an outer was not as sharp as a major's, so Lexi couldn't make out the sea. To her, the end of the land, the sea and the clouds on the horizon merged into an indistinct grey.

Standing in front of three of Richard's golfing friends, Troy asked, 'Have you heard of the group, Mercury Splash?'

Only one responded. 'Yes. Do I get a prize?'

The others laughed.

'Would Richard have liked them?'

'Possibly. He was a bit crazy like that. Acting younger than his age.'

'So, he might have gone to one of their concerts?'

'Possibly,' the same friend repeated.

Troy scanned all their faces. 'But you don't know for sure.'

'No.'

'Okay. Where was he on the weekend of the twenty-sixth and twenty-seventh of April?'

'He said he was going on a fishing expedition.'

'At sea or in a river?'

'Could have been either. He did both.'

'With … ?'

'Solo.'

'Where?'

'He didn't say. Anyway, knowing Richard, he'd probably change his mind twice before he got there. He was a bit unreliable like that. Shooting off all over the place.'

'Oh?'

'He'd got restless feet.'

'It wasn't to do with furniture making, then?'

'Sometimes. He went to art and craft shows. That sort of thing. But he was always after a thrill, finding a new challenge.'

'And he did all this on his own?'

His friends exchanged a smile. 'He didn't take us, that's for sure.'

'Are you saying he met up with someone else?'

Another hesitation. 'If he did, he never told us.'

Troy changed the topic. 'Have any of you been unwell in the last week?'

All three shook their heads. 'Nothing that kept us off the greens.'

# SCENE 14

*Thursday 8th May, Evening*

This time, the car sped northward, straight past Shepford, on its way to Pickling. Receiving a message from Tight End Crime Central, Lexi groaned.

'What is it?'

'Exactly what we already know. Listen. *Jon Drago Five is the drummer in a criminal group called Mercury Splash. We've listened to the music and concluded that he and his fellow musicians should be locked up immediately and permanently.*'

Troy cringed. 'That's all we need. Police officers with a sense of humour.'

'Sort of sense of humour. I'm not exactly rolling around uncontrollably.'

'No. Nor me. Have our funny friends dug up anything else yet?'

'He doesn't have a police record. Not a known trouble-maker. They're still working on it.'

'Good.'

Lexi updated Jon Five's entry on her spreadsheet and then summarized it aloud for her partner's sake. 'Jon Drago Five. Works with mercury. Easy access to mercury if he fiddles the figures. Drummer with Mercury Splash. He's been to Pickling where, in Keaton Hathaway's flat, we found a hair belonging to someone who's been exposed to mercury. The hair matches Jon Drago Five's for length and colour. He works in the Tight End area where one of our victims – Alyssa Bending – went before she got sick. With his group, he's been to Shepford where another one of our victims lives – Miley Quist. She may well have gone to his gig. No obvious connection to Richard Featherstone.'

'No obvious motive either,' Troy muttered.

'But is all that enough to commandeer a sample of his DNA?' Answering her own question, Lexi said, 'Borderline.'

Eager to advance the investigation, Troy said, 'I reckon I could justify it.'

'I'll send it through to our funny friends up north and see if they'll do it.'

Troy nodded.

'Talking of justify,' Lexi added, 'that's the name of the insect farm where Keaton Hathaway worked. The one we're about to visit.'

'Justify?'

'Yeah. Short for *Just Insects For You* – or Just-i-f-y.'

Troy pulled a face. 'What is it about this case? The Doom Merchant, Mercury Splash, and now insect breeders dreaming up a rib-tickling name.'

'We're bugged by comedians,' Lexi replied with a smirk.

Troy squirmed in his seat. 'Don't you start.'

Justify was housed in a low but large wooden structure, built in a field to the west of Pickling. The owner, Yasmin Nadya One, seemed eager to show her visitors around. First, she took them into a warm and humid room, as big as a warehouse, where she grew twenty million mealworms in white plastic trays placed in a vast array of racks.

'If you put them in wooden boxes,' Yasmin said, 'they'll just eat their way through the wood.'

Troy peered into a tray and grimaced. The worms formed a wriggling mass around some pieces of potato.

Yasmin smiled at Troy's expression. 'They're great. Not a pretty sight, perhaps, but very versatile.' She put her hand into the tangle of live worms and stirred them around. 'If you throw in some apple, they come out tasting of apple.'

Despite the stifling conditions, Troy shivered.

As an outer who loved her food, Lexi looked to be in heaven.

'We're very careful with feed,' Yasmin told them. 'If you let them feed on waste, poisons can build up in their bodies. Then they'd be useless for human consumption.'

'Have you ever had a problem with mercury pollution?' Troy asked.

'No. We only use the best quality feed. No contamination whatsoever.'

'It's hot in here.'

'That's how the worms like it.'

'Do you have mercury thermometers?'

'No. It's all controlled electronically these days.'

'Any other sources of mercury?'

'No, not that I'm aware of.'

Talking to Lexi, Troy said, 'When you tell me that outers keep the fly population down, it's not true. You're making as many insects as you eat. You're not just eating the nuisances out there.' He nodded towards the exit.

'You don't want to eat what's flying and crawling around all over the place. You don't know where it's been.'

Yasmin laughed. 'She's right. It's like I just said. The ones outside might be tainted. Plenty of people do eat them, but there's a risk. They might have been feasting on excrement. You wouldn't really fancy popping that into your mouth, would you?'

'I'll stick with sausage and chocolate.'

'But they contain insects as well. The law permits up to sixty insect fragments in one hundred grams of chocolate. And, as for sausages, you don't know what … '

Troy put up his hand to stop Yasmin. 'Lexi goes on and on about that – three times a day.'

Yasmin grinned. 'Come on. I'll show you the crickets in the next part of the building.'

Almost as soon as he walked through the door, Troy felt a scrunching noise under his foot.

Yasmin One shrugged. 'You've stepped on a cricket making its bid for freedom. I won't miss it much. I've got thirty million more in here.'

A loud high-pitched chirping filled the massive room. Large white pens were stacked from floor to ceiling. Peeping inside one of them, Troy and Lexi saw thousands of brown insects crawling madly all over each other.

'I grow them on cardboard egg boxes. They hatch and live there for six weeks or so, stuffing themselves with pure grain, before I harvest them. They're gassed, washed in hot water and ground or baked at the processing unit.'

'This is the operation that Keaton Hathaway managed?' asked Troy, raising his voice above the crickets' shrill.

'Yes. I'm really sorry to lose him.'

'And you're sure your crickets haven't ever poisoned any of your customers – or your workers?'

'I wouldn't still be in business if they had,' Yasmin replied. 'I'd be shut down at the first hint of contamination – or if anyone complained.'

'What did you think of Keaton?'

'He was a nice man, slightly awkward with people. But … '

'What?'

'He was a major. He didn't share our passion for insects.'

'Slightly awkward,' Troy repeated. 'In what way?'

Yasmin shrugged. 'I got the feeling he was happier with rocks and fossils than he was with living people. Or living insects for that matter. I don't think it was because he was a major in a workplace dominated by outers. I'm sure that didn't bother him. It's just that he preferred dead things.'

'Did you keep track of where he went, chasing rocks and fossils?'

She smiled. 'Impossible. Anyway, he kept himself to himself. It would have felt like an intrusion to ask him what he was up to. But I bet he would have opened up if anyone around here shared his interests. But geology isn't our thing.' She shrugged again. 'We're all mad keen on biology and entomology instead.'

'Well, how about his latest – his last – trip?'

She shook her head. 'Sorry.'

'Did he get on okay with the other men who work here? How about an outer with silvery hair, brown eyes, maybe taller than usual?'

Yasmin thought for a moment. 'That doesn't match anyone here but, yes, he was fine with everyone – in his own way. There was certainly no hostility. I like a happy, harmonious business and that's what I've got.'

'What about music? Do you know if he was into it?'

'As I said, he kept himself to himself.'

'So, you didn't hear him mention a group called Mercury Splash?'

'No.'

Troy nodded. 'Thanks.'

'Do you want to see the rest of the farm? Ants, termites, scorpions ... '

Troy put up both hands. 'I think we've seen enough and asked you all we needed to.'

The two detectives made their way back to Justify's car park. With a sigh, Lexi did not hide her disappointment that they'd refused to finish the farm tour. Troy did his best to hide his relief.

# SCENE 15

The car slowed as it negotiated the busy road that led to the electronics company called Switcher and, beyond it, to central Pickling. Both Troy and Lexi looked to the left where the security lights mounted on Pickling Prison's walls dispelled the dusk.

'We can stop here for a bit, if you like,' Lexi said. 'I don't mind.'

Troy glanced at the illuminated prison and then turned his head away. 'We've still got things to do. Important things.'

Lexi glanced sideways at him. 'Okay. It's up to

you.' She didn't alter the car's instructions and it continued towards Switcher.

Fifteen minutes later, the car turned left where two flattened squirrels lay dead in the road. It rolled gently down a drive to the company's main entrance. Inside, the manager took Troy and Lexi to a secure storeroom at one corner of the building. Opening it with a code, she led them into the plain windowless chamber. Using a key attached to her uniform, she unlocked a cupboard that bore a hazard warning sign.

'There you go,' she pronounced. 'Our stock of mercury. All safely stowed away according to chemical regulations. Double-locked.'

Troy nodded. 'But it doesn't just stay here. You bring it in and take it out to make switches with it. Have you ever lost any?'

'Not a significant amount.'

Lexi pounced. 'What do you mean by that?'

'Well, no process can be one hundred per cent efficient,' the outer replied. Smiling, she added, 'When you eat a cricket cookie, you always lose the odd crumb.'

'How much mercury has gone astray?' Lexi asked bluntly.

'A few milligrams with every operation. In terms

of health and safety, an almost insignificant amount.'

'Almost,' Lexi repeated.

Troy interrupted. 'What's that noise?'

Above their heads, there was a faint scratching sound. It stopped as soon as they all began to listen.

The manager shook her head with annoyance. 'Oh, there's a squirrel farm across the way. It's supposed to be secure but it isn't. They're crafty little creatures. They get everywhere around here. Quite a few that escape come in our direction. They make up almost all the road-kill. Some that get across the road find their way under our eves. They're a nuisance. They nest in the roof space and chew wood, electric cables and insulation.'

'Do they come down here – into the places where your people work?' Troy asked.

'I've never seen them, but one or two of my staff have reported sightings.'

Troy and Lexi exchanged a glance.

'Does the farm supply squirrel meat for majors?' said Troy.

'Squirrel pies and that sort of thing.' The manager grimaced. Pointing upwards she said, 'Anyway, this latest batch had better make the most of it tonight.'

'Why?'

'Because the pest controller's coming back in the

morning. That'll be the end of them – till the next lot of escapees look for lodgings.'

Troy nodded. 'What time are they coming? The pest controllers, that is.'

'Early. At first light, they said.'

'We'll be here,' he replied.

In the warm night air outside Switcher, Troy said, 'This could be making sense.'

Walking back towards the main road, Lexi replied, 'Yeah. A few squirrels jaywalk across the street and take up residence at Switcher. They forage around the factory, pick up mercury and stagger back to the farm. They're slaughtered before the mercury kills them and, hey presto, they end up in pies – which end up in majors.'

'Thousands of squirrels go into thousands of pies and almost all of them are fine,' Troy said, 'because they're made with unpolluted squirrels that haven't left the farm. But maybe just a few squirrels have been in Switcher – where there's some mercury on the loose – and they make a few contaminated pies. Like four in the last couple of weeks.'

'That'd explain why there hasn't been a mass poisoning.'

'Exactly. Four poisoned pies get sent out to shops

or restaurants and are eaten by four random majors.'

Lexi smiled. 'Not a human multiple murderer but four pesky squirrels.'

'It fits. A tidy explanation.'

'We'll see.'

'I suppose analysing the stomach contents of our victims won't help.'

'No,' Lexi replied. 'If it's food that caused the trouble, it will have gone through them before symptoms set in.' She paused before adding, 'But I need to look at concentrations of mercury in contaminated squirrels – and see if it's enough to kill an adult major. I'm not going to wait till morning. There's something I can do right now. I'm going to analyse some road-kill. They'll have the equipment I need in Pickling Crime Central.'

'I'd better tell my grandma I'm stuck here. She'll be delighted. Then I'll find a bed for the night.'

'Yeah. You go and get some sleep. I've got some serious scraping to do.' Lexi extracted a pair of latex gloves and a couple of evidence bags from her pocket.

# SCENE 16

*Thursday 8th May, Midnight*

Troy stood across the road from Pickling Prison and trembled. He wasn't cold. The night was mild and the southerly breeze was warm. Something about the quiet, grim building made him shudder. Troy's sight had adjusted to the dark, so the glare from the security lamps stung his eyes. The brightness outside the prison suggested shadowiness within. It was the darkness behind the light that troubled him. He lingered, watching and wondering. Wondering what his father was doing and how he was coping.

Was Winston Goodhart asleep or lying restlessly

on an uncomfortable bunk, thinking about his life, his wife and his son? How was he treated by the other prisoners? How was he treated by the guards? What was the food like? What colour was his hair now? Or had he gone bald? Did he have his head shaved? If he walked out right now, would Troy recognize him? How did he pass the time? Did he get to kick a ball around some exercise yard?

Troy remembered playing football with his dad – at least, playing with a football in the garden and a park. But perhaps Dad had done that only for his son's sake. Perhaps Winston Goodhart didn't like football. Troy sighed and stared for a moment at the ground. He didn't even know if his own father liked football. He should know that – and a lot more.

He looked up again. Once this case was over, maybe he'd come back to Pickling. Maybe then he'd find the courage and forgiveness to visit prisoner Goodhart.

An hour after he trudged away, a grey squirrel nesting behind a cupboard in the prison kitchen bit through a cable and electrocuted itself. The live wire sparked and set fire to the animal's dry bedding. The flames spread to the cupboard itself and the cooking oil inside. That was the start of a catastrophic chain of events.

A thin wisp of smoke rose from the rear of the prison and dispersed in the breeze. It seemed innocent, like the vapour trail of an aeroplane decorating the sky. No one outside took any notice. Inside, a smoke alarm sounded but, in the dead of night, the response was slow. When it came, it was too late. The kitchen was already ablaze and the flames were ready to spread.

# SCENE 17

*Friday 9th May, Dawn*

As soon as Lexi saw Troy in the harsh morning sunlight outside Switcher, she shook her head. 'Those squashed squirrels didn't have a significant concentration of mercury in them.'

Troy shrugged. 'That might still fit. Maybe some big fat tyre splatted them before they got here for a mercury meal.'

'Yeah. It's still a useful result. A background reading. Any poisoned squirrel would have to have a lot more than those two.'

'A lot more and it'd be dead.'

'Mercury takes a while to kill. It could live long enough to get into a pie,' Lexi answered. 'Anyway, I need samples from the live ones in the attic – to see if they've absorbed mercury.'

They both looked towards the main road. They could see the roof of the squirrel farm, flying a bright blue flag. A yellow van with a big black rat painted on the side announced the arrival of two pest controllers.

One of them walked over to the corner of the building where the infestation had been reported. She peered at the ground for a few moments and then called out, 'It's squirrels all right. I can see some droppings. Get the traps and bait them.'

Her mate yelled back, 'I'm on it.'

The first pest controller went up to the detectives and said, 'The droppings are distinctive. Like a brown rat's but rounder, one-and-a-half to two centimetres.'

'They're clever,' Troy said. 'Must be difficult to catch.'

With a cheeky smile, she replied, 'Hey, we're outers. We can outwit any furry creature.'

'And non-furry ones,' Lexi replied, nudging her partner.

Outers were more evolved than majors. Over the years, they had lost some strength because they'd led the invention of tools – from axes to giant earth-movers – that took care of physically demanding tasks. They also became intelligent ahead of majors. Their brain size increased. Their women opted for motherhood later in life to maximize their careers, and their babies' head sizes caused more and more difficulties during childbirth. Their population crashed. Then they invented something to solve that problem too. They outsourced their reproduction to an artificial womb where eggs were fertilized and infants were incubated. This proved so popular, the change became irreversible. Female outers lost the ability to carry a pregnancy.

'Squirrels look cute,' the controller said, 'but they're rodents. Vermin, pests. Once we've got this lot caged, we'll destroy them – humanely of course.'

'I'll take them away for analysis,' Lexi said.

'Fair enough.'

Lexi grabbed her vibrating life-logger and read the confidential message that she had just received. While the pest controllers went towards the entrance to set up their traps, Lexi glanced at her partner.

'What is it?' Troy asked.

'I'm sorry, Troy. You've just been relieved of this case – at least for the moment.'

'What?' he exclaimed.

'They've asked me to break some bad news. You're wanted urgently at Pickling Hospital.'

'Why? What's going on?'

As an outer, Lexi didn't have parents and didn't understand their value, but Troy belonged to a different species with different ideas. She gulped and said, 'It's your father.'

# SCENE 18

*Friday 9th May, Morning*

Gazing at his unconscious father in the sterile room, Troy still didn't know the colour of his hair. It had burnt away. Much of his face was covered with dressings. One bare arm was landscaped with bruises and blisters. He was breathing only with the aid of a machine, and a monitor registered his weak heartbeat with bleeps.

Troy wasn't sure what he felt. Mostly, it was a mixture of anger and fear. He wasn't sure what to do. Should he hold his dad's hand? Should he say something? Would his dad be able to feel or hear anything? The outer doctor thought not. But the major son thought there would still be something inside this broken man, some unseen connection to the world.

'Hello, Dad,' he said. 'It's me. Troy.'

Did his father's heartbeat quicken just a tiny bit? Troy liked to think so.

'Gran's on her way. That's what the hospital said. They're racing her here.'

He stood beside the bed and listened to the hissing of a pump that was forcing air into his dad's unwilling, smoke-damaged lungs.

'I'm sorry I never got around to visiting. I wish ... ' He sighed and started again. 'Did you know I'm a detective now? Did Gran tell you? Two cases down, working on number three. You'd be ... interested. It's going well. North of well.' Doing his best to smile, he added, 'Though, we might be chasing a bunch of squirrels this time.'

His phone throbbed with an incoming call. Troy felt guilty to take it under the circumstances, but the screen announced it was from the police commander. He turned to one side and whispered, 'Troy Goodhart.'

'I'll be brief, Troy. You have other things on your mind. I've spoken to your dad's doctor and I understand there's little time left. I'm truly sorry. As a result, I've consulted the highest legal authorities. Given the need to act quickly, we've made an immediate decision and I'm going to confirm it in writing for you. As soon as you get it, I want you to be my representative in Pickling and read it to your father.'

Unnerved, Troy replied, 'I'm not sure he'll … '

'Have faith, Troy. Read it anyway.'

'All right.'

Bemused, Troy turned back to the eerily still patient stretched out on the bed, connected to the world by tubes and wires. Apart from his obvious wounds, he looked fit. Perhaps it was true what an undercover police officer had told Troy: there's not much to do in prison apart from working out in the gym.

'Do you still kick a ball about? Do they let you do that in prison? Prisoners versus the guards. Or would that be asking for trouble?' Troy paused. 'I was south of hopeless at school. Square peg in a round hole. I couldn't do all that clever, outer stuff. But the teachers noticed I always seemed to know what was in someone else's mind. They called me perceptive. They did some tests, decided I was good at talking to people and working them out. They thought I'd make a good police officer – with an outer partner. So, here I am. Detective Goodhart.' He spread his arms. 'Just like you and Mum.'

Troy's skills of perceptiveness and easy conversation had no value in that hospital room. He couldn't be perceptive with a stranger who was completely inert. There was no reaction to guide him. If his father heard – and understood – what Troy was saying, would he be proud and happy? Troy didn't know. Not even the heart monitor provided a response. Troy might be good at talking to people, but only when he got something back. In this one-way conversation, he felt awkward and tongue-tied.

He tried to imagine being locked helplessly in a cell as flames churned inevitably down the corridor, the heat became unbearable and clouds of lethal smoke swirled in through the vents. At least that was how he pictured his father's fate. He didn't know any better because he hadn't been given any details.

'It must have been awful,' Troy muttered. 'Someone must have let you out.' He shook his head. 'If only they'd done it sooner.'

Troy talked about living with Gran and working with Lexi Iona Four. He talked about his investigations – his successes and frustrations – and mercury. 'It's a weird runny metal. A wolf in sheep's clothing. It's fun – all bright and silvery and harmless – but it causes all sorts of bother if it's let loose. It changes into deadly stuff.'

Making Troy jump, Gran burst clumsily through the door and let out a cry. With barely a glance at Troy, she dashed to her son's bedside, clutched his left hand in both of hers and mumbled, 'Oh, honey ... '

Normally when Troy looked at his grandmother, he saw a strong woman. A woman who would never show any sign of weakness. Physically, nothing had changed, but right now Troy saw a frail ghost of his grandma. And she seemed to fade further as she stared at her sickly son, deathly pale and unresponsive. His plight was draining the strength from both of them.

She looked up at Troy. 'Has he said anything?'

Troy shook his head.

'They told me they could open all the cells at the push of a button,' Gran said to Winston. 'That's what happens in an emergency like a fire. So, what went wrong? How did you get like this?'

Troy felt the vibration of his life-logger. For an instant Gran scowled at him from across the bed because he wasn't paying attention to the last moments of his father's life. Head down, Troy didn't spot her expression. He swallowed as he scanned the message and felt his spine shiver. Looking up again, he said, 'I've got something from the police commander. It's not what I expected. Erm … I think you'd both better hear it. He wants me to read it out.'

Gran looked puzzled.

Troy steeled himself and said, 'I hope you're getting this, Dad. It's … important.'

Winston Goodhart did not react but, sensing Troy's sincerity and urgency, Gran nodded reassuringly at him.

Troy cleared his throat and spoke loudly, in case it helped his dad to hear. *'I will get straight to the point. What I am about to tell you rests on two facts. I know your state of mind was deeply affected by your wife's death and this may have influenced your conduct afterwards. Secondly, in the last few hours, you have acted gallantly and without thought for your own safety. By all accounts, you could have left the prison like everyone else, but you alone chose to go back into danger and rescue an injured prisoner. In doing so, you saw two trapped guards in even greater peril. The details are not yet clear but, once you had carried out the prisoner, you went back inside and, showing immense physical and mental strength, you freed the two prison guards and dragged them to safety. We do know that you were struck by falling masonry, suffered many burns and breathed in too many toxic fumes. For your bravery and selfless acts of the highest order, the state ... '* Troy hesitated, sniffed and blinked. 'I really hope you can hear me, Dad.' He took a deep breath to get him through the final two sentences. *'The state pardons you of all crimes. You are a free man.'*

There was silence in the room, apart from Gran's sobs and the beeping of Winston's heart monitor. Then, after seven seconds, the monitor stopped and let out a continuous, forlorn howl. The regular spikes on the screen came to an abrupt end.

Troy lowered his eyes, ashamed. The state had forgiven his dad before he had.

# SCENE 19

Considering her partner's fragile state, Lexi did not make a cutting comment about his choice of meatballs for lunch. In The Hungry Human, she watched him eating them without his usual relish. 'So, your grandma almost threw you out the house?'

'Sort of. She needs some time and space on her own and she said she was fed up of me moping around. Said Dad would want me to get on with it.' Troy smiled weakly. 'She's not a ghost any more.'

'Sorry?'

'She looked like a ghost on Friday and yesterday. She looks more like Gran today, even though she's putting on a show of strength for me.'

'There's no such thing as ghosts,' Lexi said, 'but I guess I know what you mean.'

'She's trying to battle through, so I should as well.' Troy drank some blueberry juice. 'Has your spreadsheet joined the dots yet? You'd better bring me up to speed.'

'The chief offered me a new partner. Huh. Know what I said?'

'No.'

'Yeah. That's exactly what I said. I said no. I don't know what came over me. I told them I'd only work with you.' She shrugged. 'I must be crazy. I said I'd wait for you because no one's in immediate danger – as far as we know.'

The deep-fried spiders had been placed on her plate so that they appeared to be chasing each other in an endless circle. The legs of each tarantula were crunchy but the abdomen oozed bitter brown goo.

'You'll have carried on with the forensics, though.'

'Yeah. The Switcher squirrel squatters first. They picked up some mercury for sure, but a fully grown major would have to eat about ten of them to get a lethal dose.'

'Maybe the last lot had ten times more, so one in a pie would be enough.'

'But ten times more would kill a squirrel pretty quickly. I'm not ruling it out, but it'd have to run back to the farm and get slaughtered before the mercury finished it off.'

'Okay. It's south of certain but it's still our best shot – unless you're about to tell me something that beats it.'

'Tight End Crime Central reported in on Jon Drago Five. They've been through medical records and asked around. No evidence of any of his contacts getting ill – not with symptoms of poisoning anyway. And they've drawn a blank with him running a black market in mercury.'

Troy tried to stay focused. 'I need something positive to make me feel better.'

Lexi smiled and tucked into another tarantula, making him wait. Then she said, 'We've done the isotope analysis on that hair. We can't use the result in court, but it's interesting.' To turn up the tension yet more, she took a few seconds to drink some wine. 'Whoever it belongs to, they've been eating and drinking way up north. The hydrogen and oxygen isotope ratios match very well. Easily within error limits.'

'You mean the person who probably ripped the pages out of Keaton's diary could live in Loose End or Tight End?'

She nodded. 'Or other places up there.'

'That's another reason to get a DNA sample from Jon Drago Five.'

'The locals have already done it.'

'And?'

'You said you only wanted positive results to make you feel better.'

'Oh.'

'Yeah. It doesn't match the hair.'

Troy groaned. 'We're back in the starting blocks.'

'Not quite. We know we want to speak to a northern outer with mercury-coloured hair and probably brown eyes. Okay,' Lexi said, 'it's not super-precise, but it's something.'

'True.' He wasn't in the mood for arguing or ribbing her about forensic science, spreadsheets or anything else.

'All we need is a way forward,' said Lexi.

Troy wasn't really in the mood for working out a way forward either, but he did his best. 'The squirrels are still leading the pack, so we should email Alyssa Bending's, Miley Quist's and Richard Featherstone's families. Did they like squirrel pie – or something else with squirrel in it? Keaton Hathaway's more of an unknown quantity. Let's find out where he shopped. Did he buy squirrel meat? If that gives us four positives, it could be our connection.'

'I'll do it,' Lexi volunteered. 'The next best link is Jon Drago Five and Mercury Splash. We know Alyssa went to the band's home territory – she could have bumped into him – and we know the band went to Miley's and Keaton's towns.'

'We need to figure out if Richard's done anything to give us the complete set.'

'Then there's the Tight End area. The north. Alyssa went to the fish breeding centre and the Doom Merchant in Tight End. And we know someone from the same area – not Jon Drago Five – handled Keaton's diary.'

'So, have Miley and Richard got a link to the north?'

'Good questions,' Lexi said. 'How do we find the answers?'

'I don't know about Miley,' Troy replied. 'She's tricky. But Richard went to art and craft fairs. If there's someone who organizes them up north, I guess we want to speak to him or her.'

'I'll see what I can do.'

# SCENE 20

*Sunday 11th May, Afternoon*

The responses to Lexi's messages about squirrel meat soon arrived. Richard Featherstone's wife was first. *It was Richard's favourite food. Or so he told me.* Next, Miley's father replied. *Miley ate anything – usually in a hurry. Squirrel disappeared as quick as any other meal put in front of her.* Mr Bending also sent a message. *Alyssa was keen on squirrel stew.*

Half an hour later, a police officer in Pickling answered Lexi's request for information on Keaton Hathaway's shopping habits. She read the report and then said to Troy, 'We've got records from a supermarket about what Keaton bought and, yes, it includes two lots of squirrel meat in the last three weeks.'

'That's a full house, then,' Troy replied.

'Yes. My spreadsheet's flashing *squirrel meat* at me. It thinks that's the fatal connection. But we can't put squirrels on trial.'

'Corporate manslaughter, isn't it?'

'By squirrels?' Lexi said with a grin.

'No. By corporations.'

'Switcher or the squirrel farm?'

'Possibly both. They've been north of untidy.'

'Huh. We've got no proof they're responsible for the deaths – and no way of getting it, as far as I can see. Even if we found out all four victims ate squirrel from the Pickling farm, the poisoned meat's long since gone.'

Troy nodded and sighed. 'The defence would say it's a coincidence and we've got nothing definite to pin on them.'

'That's that, then.'

Troy was not the sort to give in, but he felt inclined to agree. Right now, he didn't have the grit to put up a fight.

'These art and craft fairs up north,' Lexi said. 'Most of them are organized by an arts group. I've contacted the secretary and he's given me a number for the man who runs a monthly fair in Loose End. Horatio Vines. You might want to speak to him.'

'Yes,' Troy replied, without his normal enthusiasm.

They soon set up a video call and, after introducing himself, Troy asked, 'When was the last art and craft show in Loose End?'

'Now that's simple,' Horatio answered in a pompous accent. 'On the morning of Sunday the twenty-seventh of April.'

'What sort of art and crafts are on display?'

'Jewellery's very popular. Especially gold.' He fingered a gold pin on the lapel of his formal jacket. 'Painting, wood-turning, children's toys, home-made food, clothing and bag making. That's not an exclusive list, but it covers the majority of my exhibitors.'

'Was a man called Richard Featherstone there?'

'Well, I wouldn't know the names of the visitors, of course, but there wasn't a stall-holder of that name.'

'I'm putting up a picture of Richard Featherstone. Does that help?'

'Now that's different. I do recognize him, yes. Absolutely. He came to the fair and asked to see me. That's definitely the gentleman concerned. He told me he was a craftsman but didn't have anything to display. Instead, he asked me to put out a few business cards advertising … what he did.'

'Furniture-making?'

'Yes, that's it. I don't have any of his cards left to verify that, but he certainly made furniture.'

'Was he on his own?'

'It was just the two of us when he talked to me.'

'I'm putting three more photos on-screen. Were any of these people with him?'

'Well, now you mention it … '

Troy sat bolt upright. 'What?'

'Yes,' Horatio Vines said. 'I saw him with her. The middle photo.'

'Alyssa Bending.'

'Her name doesn't mean anything to me, but the picture has stirred a memory. After he spoke to me, I'm fairly sure I saw him strolling around the other stalls with that lady.'

Troy glanced at Lexi before replying, 'How did they seem? Like an established couple – or two people who'd just met?'

'Now that I'm not sure. But, if I recall, they seemed … close.'

'Thanks. That's very helpful.'

'Can I ask the nature of your enquiry?'

Troy smiled faintly. 'It'd be best if you didn't.' He ended the call and faced his partner. 'If he's right,' Troy said, 'we've just turned a corner.'

'If you mean it's a new twist, yeah, I agree.' She shook her head and then smiled mischievously. 'Doesn't sound like a fishing expedition to me.'

'No. But if Richard and Alyssa were having an affair, it explains what they did with their phones. And why.'

'Does it?'

'They would've called each other or texted, arranging their get-togethers. There'd be a record of it on their mobiles. I guess they both decided to hide it from their families when they got sick, not wanting to stir up even more hurt. They took their secret to the grave. Richard wiped his and Alyssa … '

'Yes?'

'Imagine you're sick,' Troy said. 'The only thing you can do is lie on a bed or struggle to the bathroom now and again. You want to get rid of your phone to save your family from knowing what you've been up to. What do you do?'

'Okay. I'm onto it,' Lexi replied.

'Onto what?'

'The water authority.'

Troy nodded. 'You agree, then. She'd have flushed it down the toilet.'

'If they find it in the sewer, I'll ask Terabyte to see if he can get any data out of it.'

Wincing, Troy said, 'As long as you don't give it to me, I don't mind.'

'His sense of smell is less than yours. And he'll know how to clean it up without ruining it.'

'If it's not already ruined.'

'Right. We've placed two of our victims up near Loose End and Tight End before they became ill. Probably together. Keaton Hathaway's got a connection to the same area through the hair stuck on his last diary. Perhaps he went up there as well. But what about Miley?'

Troy shrugged. 'Her father said she'd been swimming. That's not much to go on. Hang on ... '

'What?'

'He saw her washing her swimming costume, but that's not all. He said she cleaned mud off her trainers.'

Lexi jumped up. 'Let's go. And hope she wasn't too thorough. I want some of that mud.'

Back in the laboratory, Lexi extracted a small amount of caked soil from deep in the tread of Miley Quist's trainers. She examined it under a microscope, logging in particular the quartz grains and other minerals.

When she'd finished, she looked up at Troy and smiled. 'You won't find this combination of minerals anywhere around Shepford,' she told him. Consulting a database of soil types, she added, 'But you would in the north.'

'Really?'

'Yeah.'

'Could it only have come from there?'

'Realistically, yes. There are a couple of other similar mixes in other places, but they're outside the error limits. I can't be a hundred-per-cent certain, though. If I'm analysing layers of mud from different places she's been to, that'd blur the result. We need supporting evidence.' She hesitated. 'But I'm thinking about that. I can put it in for organic analysis and I'm wondering about doing a DNA profile on it. That'd identify any soil bacteria and fungi. Maybe that would narrow it down a bit more.'

'Good idea.'

'We'll see.'

Troy sighed. 'I just wish we had more of a handle on Keaton Hathaway's travels.'

'The team looked into all the obvious stuff.' Lexi shrugged helplessly. 'No tickets or anything useful.'

'I'm sure I'm missing something.'

'You've been distracted. Probably still distracted.'

Troy wasn't going to admit it, but his partner was right. After years without his dad, Troy might have been on the verge of accepting him back into his life when a pest and an electric cable intervened. What he got was a shell of a father. And for less than two hours. Not a single word. Not a single reaction. Nothing. Troy felt cheated. Now, he needed the investigation to push resentment to the back of his mind, to occupy his troubled brain. But sometimes it failed and the image of his dying father and distressed grandmother slipped without warning into his head.

Unconvincingly, he said, 'I'm fine. When a case gets its tentacles around you, it's hard to escape.'

'You're a sucker for a wacky series of murders,' Lexi replied.

Troy put his forehead in his hands and groaned. When he looked up again, after a few seconds, he said, 'Alyssa Bending was in Tight End on Friday the twenty-fifth and in Loose End on the morning of Sunday the twenty-seventh. Richard was probably with her as well. So, where did they go exactly? What did they do and where did they stay?'

'I've already checked all the lodgings in the area.

Alyssa wasn't booked in at any of them.'

'What about camping? What if they just put a tent up in a field? Maybe they wanted a get-away-from-it-all, back-to-nature weekend.'

'In that case … ' She shrugged. 'We could go back and take a look.'

'Okay. But not yet.'

'Why not?'

'There's something I've got to do here in the morning.'

'Oh?'

'Something very important.'

'What's that?'

'Mark the next stage of my dad's journey.'

'You mean his funeral,' said Lexi.

'Yes.'

'That's a short journey.'

Troy disagreed. 'Believing in something beyond life helps. That way, death's not the end. There's the hope of a meeting of souls afterwards. Maybe we can make it up to each other.'

'That's sweet, but … ' For once, Lexi decided not to pursue the topic. 'We go north afterwards, then?'

'Yes.'

# SCENE 21

As the car powered past Pickling, Lexi glanced at her partner and said, 'I haven't asked. How are you feeling?'

Troy took a deep breath. 'Funerals help. You can think back to the good times. But they were a long time ago. I kept thinking about me not getting in touch.' He shook his head. 'I feel like I've just sat the most important exam of my life and when the bell went for the end, I realized I've made a complete mess of it. I got the whole thing wrong. But it's too late. I feel sick to my stomach and I've got to live with the fact that I've failed. Know what I mean?'

Lexi shook her head. 'Never had a less than perfect exam performance.' Then, trying to cheer him up, she smiled cheekily.

'Yeah. Right.'

'The more people are educated, the less they believe in religion. Outers are cleverer, so we're good at exams and we don't believe in all that business about souls and the afterlife. No evidence for either.' She shrugged. 'Anyway, going on for ever sounds boring to me. I'm happy that, when I die, that's my lot. Gone. Finished. Done.'

'Believing in heaven – a reward for living a good life – gives us a reason to behave.'

'Huh. You majors set yourselves up for guilt, shame and self-loathing, don't you? Hey. We all make mistakes. Get over it.' She hesitated, realizing that, despite trying, she wasn't being sympathetic. 'I'm sorry. But I can't change my opinion because you're feeling bad. I'm still me.'

'I know,' Troy replied. 'I don't want you to change – or say things you don't believe – for my sake. It's done. Dad's moved on. I just want to get on with the case.'

She looked at the road ahead and said, 'Well, we're going in the right direction. Perhaps.'

They drew a blank at the only campsite near Loose End but, knowing that Alyssa and Richard would have needed to hire camping equipment, they also tried an outdoor shop in Tight End. Surrounded by climbing, camping and skiing equipment, sturdy clothing and footwear, Troy showed a collection of photographs to two assistants who seemed to stick together like glue. 'Oh, yes,' the first one said. 'Him and her.' He pointed at the images of Richard Featherstone and Alyssa Bending.

'Really?' the other one replied, as she looked more closely at the images.

'Don't you remember?'

'Maybe,' she muttered.

'They looked very cosy together. Like they were going to have a good weekend.' He nudged his colleague.

She nodded. 'That's right. They asked about somewhere.'

'Yes. Somewhere to go walking and fishing.'

Troy simply stood there and listened to the two of them. He saw no need to interrupt with questions.

'Where was it?'

'He – the man – had an ancient map. It wasn't downloaded. Really old and tatty.'

'That's right. It was something about wild walks.'

'We'd never seen it before, had we?'

'That's right,' she agreed. 'I hadn't heard of the path they asked about either.'

'That's how wild it was.'

They both laughed. Then they looked at Troy and the male major said, 'So, it looks like we can't help you on where they went.'

'But it was off the beaten track,' Troy replied.

'No doubt about it.'

'Did they hire – or buy – anything other than a tent?'

'No. Just the tent.'

'The map Richard was holding. You must have got an idea about the area it covered.'

The man replied, 'It was between Loose End and the sea.'

'That's right,' his friend added. 'It's kind of wild up there. Parts of Loose End Edge used to be popular with climbers and hang-gliders.'

The first shopkeeper chipped in, 'Caving and pot-holing as well, but not any more. There was an accident. It's not safe. Landslips and the like. You'd have to be crazy to go along the edge now.'

'Richard mentioned fishing … ' Troy began.

'There's the river – and lots of streams that feed into it.'

'And two remote bays. Very hard to get to. One would be a long walk. They'd have to scramble down to the other or go by boat.'

'And if we wanted to go there now?' asked Troy.

'Take the road north from Loose End.'

'That's right,' the woman said. 'The road ends at the chemical factory. You're on foot from there.'

'What's this factory?' said Lexi.

The shop assistants looked at each other blankly and shrugged. 'It makes chemicals. That's all we know. It's out of the way because it's not very pretty.'

'And it smells.'

'Okay. Thanks,' Troy said.

On the way out, Lexi elbowed Troy and said, 'Not a very funny comedy double act.'

'Quite useful, though,' Troy replied.

Ethyl Products was the most northerly industry in the country. It sat in a remote spot in the river valley, about five kilometres from the estuary and open sea. It was a tangle of tanks, scaffolding and pipes thicker than tree trunks. And downwind there was a faint sweetness in the air.

The factory made some simple substances for the chemical trade. Other factories took those basic building blocks and turned them into useful products like plastics, medicines, perfumes and dyes. Online, Lexi discovered that Ethyl Products had been notorious. A few years earlier, the factory had switched to making acetaldehyde with a new process involving mercury sulphate. An unexpected and unwanted reaction resulted in a small amount of methylmercury. This, the most feared of the toxic compounds of mercury, was released into the river. It killed all the fish and most of the other local wildlife.

'Do you still use mercury sulphate?' Troy asked the Head of Operations.

'No. Not any more. As soon as we realized what was going on, we discontinued that process.'

'But do you still keep mercury sulphate?'

'Er … No.'

'Why hesitate?'

'I haven't been asked about it for years.'

'Is the river still poisoned?' Troy queried.

'No. We test it to make sure. I'd happily swim in it – or drink it. The habitat's fully recovered.'

Lexi and Troy left Ethyl Products and made their way towards the estuary. To either side and behind them, hills rose up and, in places, water gushed down into the valley. There was no clear path. Dragging their boots through the scrubland, they battled alongside the river. They saw no evidence that any other human beings had trodden the same route and no evidence of a pitched tent.

'It's a bit of a coincidence about Ethyl Products,' said Troy as they trudged shoulder-to-shoulder, all the time scanning ahead and to the sides.

'Yeah. But maybe not as much as you think. A lot of people used mercury till everyone realized how nasty it could be. There's probably a story like theirs almost everywhere.'

Troy gazed at the quiet countryside and said, 'It's nice out here.'

'Huh. Too much empty space.' She grinned and shielded her eyes with her left hand, 'Too much sunshine and fresh air.'

Troy stopped walking. 'What's that noise?'

'What noise?'

'That.'

There was a definite scrabbling in the bushes a few paces in front of them.

Lexi shrugged. 'A rabbit? I don't know.'

'It could be a person. Hiding.'

'Too quiet.'

A couple of frightened blackbirds flew high into the air, issuing loud warning cries.

Troy sighed. 'Okay. Not a person.'

'I'll tell you what else there's too much of.'

'What?'

'Ground. There's too much for us to cover.'

Troy nodded. 'I feel like I'm treading water. Not getting anywhere.'

'What are we going to do about it?'

Mentally drained, Troy shrugged.

Lexi pointed upwards. 'We'd be able to see a lot more – and finer detail – from up there.'

'Like blackbirds.'

Lexi took her life-logger in her hands. 'I'll see if our funny friends in Tight End Crime Central have got a drone they can send in our direction.'

'Good thinking.'

'I'll make sure it's fitted with a high-resolution camera.'

'While we're waiting, let's carry on to the estuary and look for any signs of anyone else.'

'Huh.'

'We've got this far. We might as well carry on and see if there's any hint of anybody fishing.'

'Like what?'

Troy shrugged. 'Discarded fishing line. Footprints. Anything.'

'All right.'

In twenty minutes, they ran out of land. They arrived at a small sandy bay and the sea. The spot was mostly unspoiled. The only feet that had patterned the beach were those of seabirds. There was one drinks can, partly buried in sand.

'It probably came down the river,' Lexi said. 'It's not in good condition. Corroded. It's been here longer than a couple of weeks.'

Troy nodded.

They went over to the only other object lying on the beach. At the high-tide mark near some rocks, there was a rotting fish.

Lexi squatted down by it and grimaced. 'We've come all this way for one dead fish. It doesn't mean anything. No hook in its mouth as far as I can see. It could have died of old age or got left behind in a pool. But ... ' She sighed and pulled on a glove.

'Because you're methodical ... '

'Yeah. I'm going to take it back to test it for mercury.' She slid the smelly corpse into an evidence bag and sealed it. 'I'm going to take a sample of the river water as well – just in case Ethyl Products are still pumping out pollution.'

Troy bent down, picked up a flat stone and skimmed it across the surface of the sea. It managed three bounces before a wave lurched upward and swallowed it. Overhead, two gulls screamed at each other.

'Ready to go back to civilization?' Lexi asked.

'The end of land's always a bit magical.'

'Magical?'

Knowing his partner wouldn't understand, Troy smiled. 'Yeah. I'm ready. Let's go back.'

# SCENE 22

*Monday 12th May, Afternoon*

At first, Lexi struggled to control the drone smoothly and, at the same time, remember the instructions that the police technician had hastily told her. But soon she got the hang of it and, apart from an occasional blurry image, she was successfully recording a bird's-eye view of the area.

The two detectives were sitting in a café at Loose End, surveying the rugged landscape without even moving, without breathing all that fresh air. They were able to cover far more ground far more thoroughly than when they were hiking over it. They could even zoom in on any particular area – once Lexi had mastered the software downloaded into her life-logger. But there was too much information to study in detail.

'This is the best way to appreciate the countryside,' Lexi said. 'Inside, with a beer, fudge laden with crickets, and a drone doing the hard work.'

The unmanned aerial vehicle was flying parallel to Loose End Edge. On the screen of Lexi's life-logger, they watched the movie. Vertical scars marked the positions where water cascaded down and occasional black patches were the tell-tale signs of the mouths of caves. Lexi had instructed the drone to continue its journey to the sea. That would be the limit of its range, but it would allow them to explore the second bay at a distance.

'What's that?' Troy tapped the corner of the screen.

At the base of the vertical hillside, there were boulders and something dark, obscured by surrounding trees.

'Not sure,' Lexi said, peering at the monitor. 'I'm zooming in but I still can't make it out. It's not the camera's fault. It's this screen. It's too small and the resolution's not great.' She let out a frustrated breath and said, 'I'll let the drone carry on. When it's finished the whole area, let's collect it and go back to

Tight End. We can put all the data on a large screen in Crime Central. Maybe then ... '

'Okay.'

'What we really need to do is to narrow it down,' Lexi said. 'Then we stand a chance. Right now ... '

'We're looking for the legendary needle in a haystack.'

'Something like that.'

'Actually, it's harder,' said Troy. 'We don't even know what we're looking for. The needle's a red herring. We're chasing a small unknown in a giant haystack.'

On the way to Tight End, Troy sat on one side of the car and Lexi on the other. The drone occupied the space in between them, its battery almost exhausted. But its camera had successfully transmitted huge amounts of data to Crime Central and to Lexi's life-logger. The lightweight device at her hip also vibrated twice during the journey with incoming results.

The first message came from Terabyte. Alyssa Bending's mobile had been discovered, wedged in a grating at Pullover Creek sewage works. Shepford Crime Central's expert on all things electronic had collected it and found that exposure to running water – and who knows what else – for several days had wrecked it. Summarizing, Lexi told Troy, 'Alyssa's phone was where you thought it might be, but the data in it's gone for ever according to Terabyte. Washed away. The water's corroded its chips and memory card.'

Troy nodded. 'She and Richard covered their tracks pretty well.'

Studying her life-logger again, Lexi smiled broadly. 'Here's something, though.'

'What?'

'I said we need to focus the search. Hey presto. This'll help. It's the mud on Miley Quist's trainers. I told forensics to profile all the DNA. Most of it's ordinary soil bacteria and fungi that could come from almost anywhere. Apart from ... '

'What?' Troy said again.

Lexi paused, reading ahead. 'You like fungi, don't you? Especially mushrooms. When it comes to genes, they're closer to animals than plants. The computer's highlighted one stretch of DNA from her shoes. It comes from a mushroom, *Rhodotus palmatus*, usually called the wrinkled peach because it looks like ... '

'A wrinkled peach?'

'Only if you use a lot of imagination. Anyway, the important point is that it's quite rare, apparently. Listed as endangered.'

'But Miley's stepped on one?'

'Yeah. In this country, it grows on rotting hardwood but only in two places – the extreme west of the National Forest and in woodland up here.'

Troy nodded slowly. 'That fits.'

'It means we can concentrate on wooded bits of the drone data.'

'The only problem with that is the trees. They get in the way of an aerial view.'

# SCENE 23

*Monday 12th May, Evening*

Tight End Crime Central was housed in the oldest building in the town. Standing outside it, looking at the ancient structure with its warped and weary oak beams, Lexi murmured, 'It's … '

'Full of character?' Troy suggested.

'Huh. That's not what I was going to call it,' Lexi replied with a grin. 'Worn out, perhaps. But they tell me their equipment's okay. Come on.' She led the way to the entrance.

Inside, it felt like hang-gliding. Or at least like a hang-gliding computer game. Troy and Lexi were standing in front of a large screen as the moving image swept over the countryside. But they didn't know if they were soaring over a crime scene or simply experiencing a virtual, exhilarating and unsettling flight over a wilderness.

'This feels weird,' said Troy. 'A white-knuckle ride without white knuckles.'

'You should do the real thing. Hang-gliding's breath-taking. The closest you'll come to being a bird.'

Keeping his eyes on the passing scenery, Troy said, 'Here's that wood with the mystery black hole.'

Lexi stopped the onward flight and magnified the image. The large boulders and trees cast shadows and stopped a lot of light penetrating the feature. Even so, Lexi said, 'It's a pool. It's got to be. See? There's a lighter patch at the top, next to the cliff. That's where it's churned up by the waterfall.'

'That figures.' Troy paused before adding, 'And we know Miley stepped on rotting wood and went swimming. Look. There's no path. To take a dip here, she'd have to go through the trees.'

'Yeah, but we're a long way from proving she was here,' Lexi said, nodding towards the frozen picture. 'She'd have to scramble over the rocks as well.'

'Exactly. That's probably what'd make it attractive. It'd be hidden from anyone in the valley. Not that there's likely to be anyone. Anyway, the stone and trees would shield it. We can only see it because we've got a bird's-eye view.'

'Let's carry on,' said Lexi. 'I want to scan the whole area.' She set the video in motion again.

The overflowing water from the secret pond ran into a brook. Downstream, some white specks caught Troy's eye. He cried out, 'Stop! What's that?'

'Not sure.'

'Like small pieces of paper floating in the water,' he said.

'Yeah.' Lexi zoomed in until the resolution neared its limit and began to blur the image. She shook her head. 'I can't make it out.'

'Nor me, but if I had to guess … '

'What?'

He studied the image some more and then answered, 'I don't know, but they could be dead fish.'

Lexi glanced at her partner and then back at the screen. 'Could be,' she stressed. 'Could be something else.'

'But if they *are* dead fish, it'd be … '

'Significant.'

'North of significant. It'd mean something happened upstream from here. Possibly a poison.

Possibly near that pond.' He looked at his partner and said, 'We need to go and see it in the flesh.'

'Yeah. Tomorrow. When we've got daylight.'

'We can see if there's any sign of Richard and Alyssa camping somewhere near. Even better if there's a trace of them fishing in the stream.'

'And I can hunt wrinkled peaches.'

Troy sighed. 'I still don't know how Keaton Hathaway fits into all this.'

'Perhaps he doesn't,' Lexi said. 'We're getting ahead of ourselves. I want to finish the film.'

'Okay.'

At the second bay, even smaller than the one they'd visited earlier, there were a few more of the white specks, but the images still did not have enough definition to identify them.

'I bet Terabyte would have a higher resolution camera,' Lexi grumbled. 'He'd enable us to count the scales on the fish, if that's what they are.'

Troy smiled.

'Anyway, that's that,' she said. 'We've flown over the whole area.'

'Methodically.'

'Yeah.'

Troy gazed at her but did not say a word.

'What's wrong?' she asked.

'I know what I'm missing now.'

'How do you mean?'

'Keaton Hathaway. He's not the type to just buy rocks and minerals. He'll have collected and logged each one himself. He's as methodical as you. That's the important point. Every single one will be in his notebooks.'

'I think I see where you're going with this.'

'Yes. If he collected any in the last couple of weeks, they'll be missing from his records. They'll be on the torn-out pages. If we find out which ones they are, they might tell us where he's been.'

Lexi nodded. 'Not bad for a major. Some minerals only come from a few specific places. Leave it with me. I need something interesting to do tonight. It'll take an age but it'll be easy because all his journals were scanned into here.' She tapped her life-logger. 'I'll check the list of his rock samples against his notes. A process of elimination will tell me if there's a mismatch.'

'Good plan.'

# SCENE 24

*Tuesday 13th May, Early morning*

Lexi couldn't wait for a sleepy major to report for duty in the morning. She went to Troy's hotel and met him in the restaurant. 'You were wrong,' she said. 'Having spent all night with Keaton's notes, I've decided he wasn't as methodical as me. He's more. Totally obsessive. I've been through all his diaries – going back years. I found lots on all his mineral samples – where he got them and when – except for one.'

Troy put down his glass of pineapple juice. 'Spit it out.'

'The gold.'

Troy nodded. 'He's not the type to miss one out, so it's got to be on the missing pages. He got it in the last couple of weeks.'

'Yeah. Gold.' Lexi smiled triumphantly. 'I've been doing a bit of research while you've been flat out in bed. It used to be extracted by dissolving it in mercury. Not any more because it's illegal and dangerous.' She raised her eyebrows.

'Where did this happen?'

'Three or four places around the country. But one of them is … '

'Well?'

'Are you ready?'

'Yes.'

'In the caverns of Loose End.'

'Ah.'

'Some of those holes in the hillside are disused gold mines, apparently. My information tells me they haven't been worked in living memory.'

'Meaning they haven't been worked officially?'

Lexi nodded. 'The mining industry pulled out when they became unprofitable – not enough gold left. It doesn't rule out someone mopping up the small amount that big business couldn't be bothered with.'

'And doing it with mercury?'

'Illegally, yes. It's a possibility.'

'So, to get a chunk of gold for his collection, Keaton Hathaway could have come up here and bumped into a dodgy outfit using mercury.'

She nodded. 'Maybe he got in their way or threatened to report them.'

'And, one way or another, he got a fatal dose of their mercury.'

'It's more believable than dodgy squirrels,' she said. 'So, swallow that fried pig's blood, grab your crampons and ropes, and we'll get going.'

# SCENE 25

*Tuesday 13th May, Early morning*

Gazing out of the window as the car approached Loose End Sports Centre, Troy snapped an instruction at the on-board computer. 'Stop here!'

Dutifully, the car pulled off the road and came to a halt.

Puzzled, Lexi said, 'What's up?'

Troy pointed to the left. 'A football pitch.'

Lexi was still bewildered by her partner's behaviour.

'So what?'

There wasn't even a proper game in progress.

Eight players were having a training session: passing, running and shooting.

'You know what I most want to do right now?' said Troy.

'Catch a poisoner?'

'Apart from that.'

'No. What?'

'Kick a ball around – in honour of my dad. It's something we did a lot when I was little. It'd make me feel better.'

'You want to play sentimental games when we're on a case?'

Troy smiled at her. 'Yes and no. I'd *like* to, but I won't because that'd hold us up. The idea helps the case, though.'

'Does it?'

He told the car to resume its program. 'Miley Quist. She loved her grandma but, like my dad, she passed away. So, what did Miley do? She did something that, according to her dad, made her feel better. She wouldn't have kicked a ball around. I bet she did something in honour of her free spirit of a grandmother. We know one thing she did was to go swimming. A special swim, I should think. Perhaps one her grandma did when she was young.'

'Yeah. But what are you getting at?'

'I think we should send a team to Miley's grandma's house. Maybe somewhere inside there'll be a photo or a map or something about a special swimming place. Maybe that place will be around here. And that's why Miley stepped on a wrinkled peach.'

Lexi nodded. 'Okay. You speak in riddles sometimes, but it eventually makes sense. I'll get onto it.'

Both of them had a backpack. In hers, Lexi had a full forensic kit from Tight End Crime Central. She had also borrowed protective gear for Troy because, as a major, he would be vulnerable to mercury poisoning. She'd put it into her partner's rucksack. Knowing they could be out in the wilds for some time, they'd packed water and food. Attached to the side of each backpack was a small machete.

Just before the car came to a halt behind Ethyl Products, Lexi checked a message from her colleagues at Tight End. She looked at Troy and said, 'Good that you've brought an overall and gloves.'

'Why?'

'The post-mortem on yesterday's rotting fish. The toxicity people tell me it had far more mercury than was good for it.'

'Couldn't that be down to Ethyl Products?'

'No, or there'd be lots more. Those blackbirds – and seabirds paddling in the bay – would be dead. Anyway, the analysis says the river water's clean. You could drink it, like the company claimed. The fish must have got poisoned somewhere else, floated out to sea and then the tide dumped it on that beach.'

Troy got out of the car and pointed to the north. 'Somewhere out there could be our murder weapon.'

'It could have been an accident. But, either way, you're the one in danger. You're the major.'

'I'll sidestep any shiny metals.'

'You can do what you like with the metal, except breathe its vapour. But that won't be an issue in the open air. Mercury compounds – probably invisible – are what you've got to avoid touching or swallowing.'

'I'll steer clear of anything invisible,' Troy said drily.

They set off towards the cliff that marked the eastern edge of the valley, in the direction of the copse and hidden pool. There wasn't a path so they had to make their own. The journey felt like a cross between walking and wading. Now and again, Lexi checked the coordinates on her life-logger to make sure they were going in the right direction. Coming up to an unruly thicket, she held a machete in her left hand

and pointed with it. 'I think we need to aim a bit more to the right.'

'Okay.'

Once they'd hiked and hacked through the bushes and brambles, Troy said, 'Let's take a break.'

'Already? You're supposed to have more stamina than me.'

'Not that sort of break,' Troy replied, reaching for his mobile. 'If there's a signal out here, I want to call Horatio Vines.' He glanced down at his phone. 'It's enough.' When he got through to the man in charge of organizing the Tight End art and craft festivals, he said, 'I want to ask about the jewellers who come to your fairs. Where do they get their gold from?'

Horatio hesitated. 'Now that's easy. They buy it, as you would expect, from legitimate gold dealers.'

'Is any of it sourced locally?'

Horatio chuckled. 'I'm not aware that the streets of Tight End are overflowing with gold.'

'But you are aware that obstructing an investigation by withholding information is an offence?'

'Yes.'

'So do you have anything to add about artists getting gold from dodgy sources?'

'No.'

Troy finished the call and said to his partner, 'He knows something about black-market gold.'

Surprised, Lexi asked, 'Did he admit it?'

'No.' Troy put his phone away and continued the trek. 'He said the people who sell stuff at his fairs buy their gold from legitimate dealers. He wouldn't say that unless he knew there were illegitimate ones. He'd just say "dealers". So he's protecting his stall-holders who've got gold from the back of an unmarked van.'

'Perceptive,' Lexi said with a smile.

The grasses, heather and brambles came up to their knees – sometimes up to their waists – and clawed at their legs, making the hike laborious. From time to time, Lexi would stop and examine the plants, looking for damage. 'No evidence of anyone else coming this way but, after a couple of weeks or so, maybe there wouldn't be any.' She glanced around. 'Anyway, someone could have walked two or three metres to either side and, in this jungle, we wouldn't spot the signs.' She pulled a long string of goose-grass away from her trousers where it had gripped like Velcro. Then it clung to her hand and sleeve. She brushed it against a shrub to get rid of it. 'Horrid stuff.' She took a drink of water and then said, 'Let's keep going. Unless you suddenly decide to make another phone call.'

'Well … '

Lexi laughed. 'Who this time?'

'No. I want to speak to the receptionist at the fish breeding centre in Tight End, but it'd be better to go and see him instead.'

'Why him?' She took a swipe at some brambles with her machete.

'He was wearing a small gold badge.'

'Him, and how many others?'

'I know. Maybe it's nothing, but … ' He glanced at her and added, 'There's no harm being thorough and methodical.'

'Huh.'

But the next call came to Lexi's phone. One of her colleagues at Shepford said, 'I think we might have what you wanted. An old booklet on hiking near Loose End – with a map. It was in a drawer at Miley Quist's grandmother's place. Someone's even marked it with a red cross and written *wild swimming* in the margin. I'll scan it and email you a copy.'

'Thanks,' Lexi replied. 'It's urgent. Can you send it to my life-logger right now?'

'It'll be on its way in five seconds. Literally.'

Lexi nodded at her partner. 'I think we're in the right place. Miley Quist's grandmother had a map of the area. I'll tell you in a few seconds.' She manoeuvred herself so she was standing shoulder-to-shoulder with her partner. That way, they could share the image.

As soon as it was transmitted, they both peered at it, unsure. Lexi zoomed in on the red cross and the comment in the margin.

'That's it,' she said. 'Look. It's the same place. It's that hidden pool under the cliff.'

The old-fashioned sketched map was very different from the drone's coloured overhead imagery. Scratching his head, Troy replied, 'Could be.'

'It was once known for wild swimming.'

'By Miley's grandma anyway.'

'Yeah. If she was the one with the red pen.'

Troy nodded. 'I bet it was different back then.' He pointed to the blank space on the map where they had left the car. 'No factory for one thing.'

'Maybe this is the same map that Alyssa and Richard had. Anyway, come on,' Lexi said. 'We might have our crime scene – at last.'

Troy stepped forward and immediately froze.

A large snake reared up in front of him. It was amber with a brown zigzag along the length of its body. Behind its head was a dark V shape. It let out a loud and long hiss.

'It's okay,' Lexi whispered. 'It's an adder.

Poisonous but not very aggressive. Painful but not fatal. Not usually, anyway. And it only strikes when it's disturbed or alarmed.'

Heart beating fast, Troy stared into the adder's eyes. 'And what is it right now?'

'Good point. Disturbed *and* alarmed. Normally they run away, but this one hasn't – so you'd better let it be the boss. Back off slowly. If you don't threaten it, it'll just slither into the undergrowth. Probably.'

Troy took a slow step backwards and the snake watched him intently.

'For a snake that's not aggressive,' Troy said softly, 'this one looks mean.'

'You invaded its personal space. What do you expect?'

He backed away some more.

The adder relaxed, sank to the ground and disappeared into the vegetation.

Troy let out a sigh.

'Let's go this way,' Lexi suggested. 'Give it a wide berth.'

'Okay.'

They made a detour around the snake's territory, not knowing if they were about to invade the space of another. Perhaps one that was even more hostile.

'That's the problem with nature,' Lexi said with a

smile. 'For every cuddly marmoset, there's a poisonous snake.'

'Given the choice, you'd prefer to be a snake handler than a monkey minder.'

'That's true,' she said. 'I like a challenge.'

They slashed at the scrubland in front of them loudly, hoping that the noise would scare away any more snakes.

They slogged northward for another forty minutes until they reached one of the freshwater brooks fed by a waterfall. They stopped and looked around.

'You know, I think we've come too far,' Troy said. He pointed upstream. 'I reckon it's up there somewhere. In amongst those trees.'

'Let's see.' Checking their coordinates, Lexi nodded. 'We must have walked past without even noticing it. But we're not too far out. We've just got to go back upstream a bit.'

'Exactly. It'll be easier walking beside the water – or paddling through it.' He nodded towards their boots. 'Waterproof shoes.'

Lexi shrugged. 'I'm an outer. I don't mind. But it might be risky for you. Let's keep to the rocks on one side or the other. But first … ' She got out her forensic kit and knelt down. 'I want a sample of the water to test for mercury back at the lab. And DNA to find out what sort of bacteria it's got.' She peered at the apparently clean water in a vial and popped it into an evidence bag. She marked the bag with the exact coordinates of the sample and stored it in her rucksack. Then she stood up.

They set out for the clump of trees at the base of the cliff and – they hoped – the secret, wild-swimming pool.

After five minutes, Troy came to a halt. 'Look.'

Lexi was already reaching for two more evidence bags and pulling on latex gloves. 'I'll collect them.' She bent down to scoop out the two small fish floating in the stream.

'From the air,' Troy said, 'they could look like pieces of white paper.'

'Maybe you were right. The thing is, what killed them?' She held them up by their tails and slid them into transparent bags. 'I'll find out. No problem.' She glanced at Troy and said, 'For now, though, it means you shouldn't go in the water. In case it's mercury.'

'If it is, it can't be Ethyl Products' doing. This is a different river. It doesn't go past the factory. It comes from the cliff, probably running through one of the caves.'

'Yeah. Where someone might be scavenging gold by dissolving it in mercury.'

Lexi was about to move on when she hesitated.

'What?' Troy prompted.

'A bit of fishing line and a hook. See?' She bagged that as well.

'Catching things here would be risky. Whoever it was didn't see any sick fish or they wouldn't have done it.'

'Maybe they weren't sick at the time, or at least weren't showing symptoms.'

Hiking beside the stream was sometimes easy, sometimes an awkward scramble over rocks. Lexi took occasional samples of water and dead fish as they went. Soon, they found themselves under the shade of trees and within the sound of tumbling water. And Lexi had something new to hunt. A mushroom shaped like a wrinkled peach.

She found it after about five minutes. A large branch of an oak had snapped off a long time ago and was slowly rotting on the ground. The fungus was growing on two different parts of the wood. While Lexi took photographs and samples, Troy gazed over her shoulder and said, 'That's supposed to look like a crinkly peach? Weird.'

'Yeah. Not very convincing. But nice in its own way.'

'More like a pink sponge.'

'I see what you mean. But more important, it's

here. Which means Miley Quist might have been here.'

Troy nodded.

'It's so distinctive to look at, I don't really need its DNA – just a photo – but I've got some anyway.'

They made their way towards the sound of falling water.

The stream was running over a large rock, about five metres high. They stood at the bottom and looked up. Positioning himself so the water did not splash him, Troy said, 'It's a giant overflowing basin. I reckon it's the wild-swimming pool up top.'

'Let's walk around it first. Find the easiest bit to climb.'

Within a few seconds, Troy came to a standstill and smiled. He wasn't looking at the rock, though. He'd spotted something among the trees. 'That's interesting.'

Lexi followed his line of sight to a small heap of charred branches. Nodding, she said, 'Someone's been here.'

Troy glanced around. 'The land's flat and smooth. Nice spot for camping.'

'And a fire's good for cooking.'

'It fits,' Troy agreed. 'Maybe Richard Featherstone and Alyssa Bending stayed here, fished and barbequed their catch. A poisonous picnic.'

'If they had a swim as well, they could've been doubly poisoned. Eating dodgy fish *and* skin absorption.'

'If they drank the water, maybe they copped it three times over.'

The detectives continued around the crag until Lexi stopped and jerked her thumb towards the rock face. 'This'll do. Look. It's not so high and there's a good few toeholds. Like a training wall. Are you up for it?'

'If you are.'

'As easy as walking up steps. Come on.' Surveying the rock, she said, 'I'll go first. Watch where I put my hands and feet, and just do what I do.'

Agile and confident, Lexi began to scale the crag as if she had Velcro on her hands and feet.

Determined not to disappoint his partner, Troy pretended to be equally confident. He dragged himself up by his fingers while his toes scrabbled for purchase. His knees scraped against the unforgiving surface. He had the stomach-churning feeling that he was about to fall backwards and land in an embarrassing and untidy heap on the ground. But he tried not to show his unease.

From above, Lexi called, 'Slow but sure's okay.'

'More slow than sure,' Troy muttered as he went

up another few centimetres. The weight of the rucksack on his back was slight but it still added to his sense of unbalance.

Already at the top, Lexi lay down and peered over the edge. 'Left hand up a bit more and to the right. There's a good grip.'

'This is the only time I've wished I was a spider.'

'Barbequed, you'd make a good meal.'

Feeling the strain in his shoulders and knees, Troy heaved himself higher.

'I'll be able to give you a hand in a minute,' Lexi said.

To hide his discomfort, he carried on talking between breaths. 'I hope this is worth it. I hope there are some suspects up there for me to question.'

Lexi looked around. 'No, but it's a nice place for a refreshing dip.'

'I've just had a thought,' Troy said, climbing within range of Lexi's dangling left arm.

'Yeah?'

'How are we going to get down?'

'The same way – but it's harder going down. Much, much harder.'

'Oh good.'

With his partner's hand gripping his right wrist firmly, Troy felt supported. He soon covered the final part and scrambled up onto the lip of the rock, joining Lexi.

There was an inviting pool of water, ideal for private swimming. Its surface wasn't a perfect mirror, though. At one side, water cascaded down the cliff and sent small ripples across the secluded pond. At the other side, the overflow spilled out. The reflection of the sky and cliff-face quivered.

Wearing gloves, Lexi took a sample of the water. 'I wish I could analyse all this stuff here and now, but I need a lab.'

To their left was one of the numerous caves in the scarred cliff. A little water dribbled out of it too. With care, they could get to it.

Noticing that Troy was eyeing the cave, Lexi said, 'I've got a torch. Fancy exploring?'

'Now we're here, we might as well take a look.'

Lexi bagged the water sample and, at the same time, extracted a powerful, handheld torch from her backpack. They had to walk very close to the edge of the rock to access the cave. It was a narrow passage between the vertical drop on one side and the pool on the other.

When they reached the mouth of the cave, Lexi turned on the torch.

Troy paused. He would not be able to go in

without trampling through running water. 'Time to get my kit on, I think.' Quickly, he slipped into the protective overalls from his rucksack. Then, together, they entered the cave, soon leaving the reassuring sunlight. The sound of running and dripping water echoed all around. Centimetres above their heads, the roof seemed to press down on them.

'Spooky,' Troy whispered. Uncannily, the word rebounded off the walls and came back to him.

'Exciting,' Lexi replied.

The light beam picked out seeping water, slime and glistening rock formations. To someone like Keaton Hathaway, the place would have been a wonderland.

As they walked forward, Lexi fanned the spotlight from side to side.

'What's that smell?' said Troy, crinkling his nose.

'Bats, I think,' Lexi answered. 'You're getting a whiff of their toileting arrangements – which are short on etiquette and hygiene.'

'It's north of disgusting.'

'Yeah. But, to be fair, if they were awake, they'd probably think we were revolting as well.'

She came to an abrupt halt as the torch illuminated something unnatural.

It was a small collection of tools. Immediately, Lexi

went over to the spot and peered at it without touching anything. A pickaxe, two sieves, a drill, three hammers, two cold chisels, several buckets, various containers, a couple of spades and two grimy hard-hats. At the bottom of two of the buckets, something metallic gleamed like silver – or mercury.

Lexi took several photographs of the hoard and each time a blinding flash illuminated the cave for a split-second.

'I want all this stuff in the lab,' she said. 'Especially the hard-hats. But … ' She looked at the bulk of the mining equipment against the size of her backpack. 'No chance. I'll need a return visit.'

'I don't think anyone climbed up here with this lot on their backs,' Troy said.

'It's not impossible,' Lexi replied, 'but I take your point.'

Troy couldn't see very far into the dark cavern, but he said, 'Maybe there's another way out – and in.'

'Huh. This isn't Shepford central zone, you know.' She flashed the torch beam down the cave to the point where it veered upwards and to the right. 'No obvious doors.'

Troy smiled. 'You never know. Maybe there's a lift around the corner.'

Lexi laughed. 'All right. Let's go and see.'

The cave was about three paces wide and, as they wandered down its length, it seemed to get narrower. Maybe it was an optical illusion. Maybe claustrophobia was making them feel hemmed in.

Troy shuddered with the cold, the dark and the damp. 'I'm glad I don't work down a mine,' he said. 'It's ... '

'Unsettling?'

He shrugged. 'Weird. Natural, but it feels unnatural to be here. Like we're invading someone else's world. Maybe it belongs to bats, not people.'

'Talking of bats ... ' Lexi said.

'What?'

'The smell's not so yucky.'

Troy nodded.

The air was fresher and their voices did not echo so much.

They carried on, aware of a slight draught and a faint, eerie glow ahead. Around the next curve, the torchlight caught a dangling rope coming from a shaft above their heads.

'Hey presto,' Lexi said. 'Not a lift, but nearly.'

Troy groaned. 'We don't have to climb all the way up a rope, do we? The rock's a Sunday stroll in comparison.'

Squinting at the sunlight a long way above them,

Lexi replied, 'No, I don't think so. There's something up there. A big basket maybe.' She pulled on the rope and the object at the top of the shaft began to descend. 'Ah. Our lift's on its way. In fact, you carry on pulling and I'll go back for those tools. At least some of them.'

Leaving Troy in the circle of daylight, Lexi dashed back to the mining equipment. She made two trips, holding as much as she could, before Troy lowered the basket to the floor of the cave. It had a crude door and space for two people. A little spare room was enough for Lexi's evidence of illegal mining.

'I think we stand in the basket and haul ourselves up on this other rope,' said Troy.

'Looks like it,' Lexi replied. 'There must be a pulley at the top. Hope you're feeling strong.'

Actually, they heaved on the rope together and the basket rose slowly and unsteadily, lurching drunkenly towards the sunshine.

Between deep breaths, Lexi said, 'You know what I think?'

'No.'

'Not perceptive enough, then.'

'What?' Troy asked.

'If this thing hadn't been used for years, it wouldn't be this smooth.'

The sunlight was getting brighter, burning their eyes.

'This is smooth?' Troy said with a smile.

'Just think what it'd be like if it hadn't moved in sixty years or more.'

'That figures.'

The basket clunked against the winch and came to a sudden halt, before it emerged from the pothole. In front of them, though, were a few rough steps cut into the rock, leading up to the grassy top of the cliff. They pulled back the door of the cage, mounted the steps and found themselves on Loose End Edge.

To the north, they could see the sea. To the south were the Ethyl Products buildings. A few paces away from the vertical entrance to the mine, they could hardly see it. The winch barely showed above ground level.

Both of them pulled on latex gloves. Then Lexi went back down to the basket and handed the mining gear, one piece at a time, up to Troy. He laid them on the grass. Lexi had already placed the two helmets in evidence bags in case any strands of hair fell out. She did not want to lose vital evidence. She called to him, 'That's the lot. Whoever's been using this pulley might've abandoned it after the deaths, but we'll see.' She held up a tiny spy camera and fixed it to the top of the shaft. Then she joined Troy on the exposed cliff.

A few metres away from the hole, there was a rough track. It went along Loose End Edge and back towards Ethyl Products. Further along, there appeared to be a long gentle slope downwards, but it wasn't suitable for a car. Lexi studied the surface of the ground. 'No tyre impressions. Probably no one's driven here for a while and the weather's got rid of any evidence.' She called Tight End Crime Central and requested an off-road vehicle to collect the buckets, hard-hats and the rest of her precious hoard.

Troy removed his protective clothing and packed it away.

Arms aching and hair buffeted by the wind, they both sat down on the grass and waited.

# SCENE 26

Crime Central's computer did not recognize the track as a road, so an automatic vehicle could not be programmed to pick up the two detectives from Loose End Edge. Instead, a driver from Tight End picked them up in a manual four-by-four. Troy smiled to himself as they bumped along the track.

'What are you grinning about?' Lexi asked him.

'You. You'll be north of happy now.' He nodded towards the rear of the jeep where the mining tools were stowed. 'You'll be able to fill a spreadsheet five times over with all that.'

'Yeah. Lots of lovely data. Is the shiny stuff at the bottom of the buckets a residue of mercury? DNA in the hard-hats. Skin or hair? When and where were they bought – and who bought them? Are there any fingerprints or were they only handled by outers? And that's just the start.'

'Busy day ahead.'

'And night,' Lexi added.

'You'll be a mine of information.'

Lexi groaned. 'I'll have some of the answers by morning. Not all.'

Troy shook his head. He felt guilty for attempting a joke one day after his father's funeral.

'Two people over to the right,' the driver announced. 'Do you want to stop?'

'Yes,' both of the detectives said at the same time.

Lexi was out of the door even before the four-by-four had fully stopped. As usual, her ability to sprint gave her the lead. With a major's superior stamina and strength, Troy would catch up only when she began to tire.

Lexi shouted, 'Stop! Detectives!'

Ahead, two girls took no notice and kept running along the edge.

Troy guessed that they were majors because Lexi was closing fast. He stumbled slightly over a rock but stayed on his feet, following his partner.

Just as Lexi reached them, one of the girls screamed and, as far as Troy could see, simply disappeared. The second girl came to a halt and Lexi dived to the ground.

Putting on a burst of speed, Troy charged towards them, guessing that the first girl had fallen down a mineshaft or a pothole. When he got there, she was dangling from the lip. The fingers of her left hand were clutching the rock but slowly slipping. Lexi was holding her right hand, but didn't have the strength or the grip to save her. The girl was panicking, kicking out uselessly with her legs. Still screaming.

Troy bent down and grasped her left wrist with both of his hands. He nodded at Lexi and together they hauled her out of the hole. They dragged her away from danger and then lowered her arms so she was sprawled on the grass, still in shock. Then they waited for the terror to subside.

The driver carefully steered the jeep, positioning it between the two girls and their escape route.

The girls shared a distinct likeness. The younger one, probably about thirteen, stood motionless and seemed almost as petrified as the girl who had fallen. She was a year or two older.

Troy plonked himself down next to her and touched her shoulder. 'You're safe. Thanks to Detective Lexi Iona Four.'

'And you,' she mumbled.

'What's your name? Both of you.'

'I'm Shea Pickup and that's my sister, Ursula.'

'You're majors?'

'Yes.'

'What are you doing here?' Troy asked.

Shea swallowed before answering. 'I … er … had a history lesson. The teacher told us they used to dig for gold here.'

'So, you bunked off school and came to see for yourself?'

'Yes.'

Troy looked up at Ursula, catching a brief expression of uncertainty on her face. 'With your sister?'

'Yes.'

'Did you find any?'

'No.'

'Nor me. But you've convinced me you don't know where the mines are.'

'How?'

'By falling down one of them.'

Shea refused to smile. She had been thoroughly

shaken by her ordeal. After all, she had been a few fingertips from death.

'Why did you run?'

'There's a *Keep Out* sign. Dangerous cliffs or something. We thought we might be in trouble.'

'That fits.' Troy gazed across the green valley for a few moments, thinking. Then he extracted a bar of chocolate from his pocket. He popped a chunk into his mouth and offered the bar to Ursula and Shea. Ursula refused but Shea took a piece. She did it automatically. Instead of eating it, she simply fiddled with it in her hand. 'Do me a favour, all right?' Troy said to her.

'What?'

'Don't come back. Seriously. It's not safe. You've found that out. And it might be even more dangerous for majors than it looks. I don't want any more people getting hurt. Okay?'

'Okay.'

Troy glanced up at Ursula. 'And you?'

Avoiding eye contact, she nodded.

'Did either of you see anyone else?'

'No. It's a bit freaky up here. All alone.'

'What's your teacher's name? And which school is it?'

'Er ... Mr Oates. Tight End High.' Shea hung her

head and muttered, 'You won't tell our parents, will you?'

'That depends.'

'On what?'

'A couple of things,' Troy said. 'First, you stay away from here.'

'What else?'

'I'd prefer not to have to go and ask your history teacher about his lesson. I don't want to waste my time – or his. So, why don't you tell me what really brought you here? If you tell me the truth, I might not have to talk to your parents.'

'Would you really go to see Mr Oates?'

Troy jerked his head towards his partner. 'Lexi's known for being thorough and methodical. She'd insist.'

Head bowed, eyes fixed on the piece of chocolate, Shea seemed surprised to see it in her hand. On auto-pilot, she put it in her mouth and sighed.

'Tell him,' Ursula said. Her voice was so hushed that the wind nearly took it away.

'I don't want to get … anybody into trouble.'

'If they haven't done anything against the law,' Troy said, 'you won't.'

Shea wiped her forehead. 'I've got a friend – an outer – and she gets all sorts of bling. You know.

Jewellery. She asked me if I wanted … but we don't have that sort of money.'

Troy needed to know the name of her friend, but he didn't ask. He didn't disrupt her flow.

Shea manoeuvred the chocolate to her left cheek and continued. 'I was … curious. So I followed her. This was days ago. Not today. She was carrying quite a big bag. Made me … even more curious. She came here. Straight past the danger sign. She met someone. A man. Quite tall with white hair. Maybe he was old. I don't know. I couldn't see. They went off along the ridge.'

'And what did you do?'

'I turned back. They'd have seen me if I'd carried on. I did a bit of online research and found out about the gold. It made sense.'

'Then, this afternoon, you got Ursula to come with you and take a look around.'

She sighed again. 'Yes.'

'And you found nothing.'

She nodded.

'What's her name? This outer girl.'

The two sisters exchanged a glance. Shea swished chocolate around her mouth without thinking or enjoying it. Ursula whispered, 'Zoe Olivia Three.'

'All right,' Troy said. 'I think we'll leave it at that.

I hope I don't have to talk to you again. Or your family. But if there's anything you haven't told me ... ' He left the threat hanging in the air.

Both girls shook their heads.

'And don't go near Zoe Olivia Three. Don't contact her. If you did, it'd be perverting the course of justice and that means more than talking to your parents. It means a prison sentence.'

Troy looked into the sisters' faces. They were both suitably sheepish. 'Okay. Let's get in the car. We'll give you a lift – and make sure you're well away from here.'

# SCENE 27

*Tuesday 13th May, Late afternoon*

While Lexi began a thorough forensic analysis of all the mining gear under the large oak beams of Tight End Crime Central, Troy headed for the fish breeding centre.

Stepping inside the warm and humid reception, with its characteristic glow and tranquil gurgling sounds from the fish tanks, Troy went up to the desk. Clearly, the receptionist remembered him from his visit last Wednesday.

'What can we do for you, Detective ... ?'

'Troy Goodhart.' He pointed to the man's lapel.

'You're wearing your gold pin again. I'm interested in it.'

'Nice, isn't it?'

'Yes. Where did you get it?'

'A craft fair.'

'Locally?'

'Yes. Loose End. Why?'

'Who sold it to you?'

The receptionist shrugged. 'No idea what he was called. But he said he runs the jewellery shop here in the shopping mall.'

'Tight End?'

'Yes.'

'Are there any other jewellers in town?'

'No. You can't go wrong.'

Troy nodded. 'Thanks.'

A familiar face greeted Troy in the jewellery shop. Horatio Vines was helping a customer to choose a bracelet. When he saw Troy, the major's expression shifted momentarily from smarmy to surly and back again.

'Ah, it's you,' Troy said. 'You run a shop as well as the fairs.'

Horatio stepped away from his customer and smiled. 'Organizing art and craft shows doesn't make me a living. I do it as a volunteer. Unpaid.'

'But you sell things at the fairs.'

'I do. It's an extension of the shop. Sometimes the punters roll up and buy a good few items. Sometimes, the right customers aren't there.' He shrugged. 'It's like the shop itself. Good days and not so good days.'

From his phone call earlier in the day, Troy was convinced that Horatio Vines was protecting someone else in the gold and jewellery trade. Perhaps someone in his own business. Troy was also convinced the culprit was an outer, unaffected by mercury poisoning, and not a major. He asked, 'Do you have an assistant?'

Horatio glanced furtively at his customer, licked his lips, and said quietly, 'No.'

The shopper's face expressed such surprise that even Horatio could not ignore it.

'Well, yes, I *had* an assistant,' Horatio said. 'No doubt he served this lady at some point. But he's no longer with me.' He glanced towards the door marked *Staff Only*.

Troy laughed. 'You're hoping he won't barge in right now and spoil what you just said. Or maybe you're working out how to sneak into the stockroom – or whatever it is – to warn him about me.' He shook his head. 'Go on. Go and get him. I need to speak to him.'

When Horatio left the showroom, Troy turned towards the shopper and asked, 'What are his prices like for pieces made with gold?'

'Very reasonable,' she replied. 'I'm impressed. Cheaper than anywhere else I've come across. I don't know how he does it.' She paused and lowered her voice. 'What's going on?'

Hearing a door slam, Troy ignored her question and dashed to the back window. Below him, a young man with silver hair – taller than himself and Lexi – sprinted across a yard, between two buildings and out of sight.

Troy closed his eyes for a moment and muttered a groan. He knew that a chase was pointless. By the time he'd found the back door, Horatio's assistant would be too far away.

Horatio came back into the showroom and said, 'Now that's unfortunate. I'm sorry but he couldn't stay. He's off duty and he's got … '

Troy put up his hand. 'Don't even try. What's his name?'

The customer, fearing a criminal connection, left rapidly without buying a bracelet or anything else.

'Nigel Edwin Thirty-One.'

'An outer.'

'Obviously.'

'I'm guessing here. Is he a scientist, an expert with gemstones, rocks and minerals?'

'He's a geologist and mineralogist. Very helpful in my line of work.'

Troy nodded. 'Brown eyes by any chance?'

'Now you mention it, yes.'

Anticipating a reaction, Troy gazed into the jeweller's face while he asked, 'Where's Zoe Olivia Three?'

Horatio's expression was genuinely blank. 'I don't know anyone of that name.'

'Okay. Show me where Nigel Thirty-One sits, relaxes or works in the staff-only area.'

Horatio hesitated.

'Or I'll arrest you for obstructing my investigation,' Troy stated bluntly.

Once Troy had seen Nigel Thirty-One's chair and a corner where he examined and polished stones, Troy said, 'Right. I'm calling in a forensic team. No one goes near here until they've finished. In fact, lock the door until they get here.'

'But … '

Troy interrupted. 'I'm still thinking about charging you with perverting the course of justice.'

'Now that's vindictive. Can you threaten me like that?'

'I don't see why not. You deserve it.'

Horatio sighed. 'All right.' Unwillingly, he added, 'I'll make sure nothing's disturbed.'

By phone, Troy also asked for a team of officers to go to Nigel Edwin Thirty-One's home and, if he wasn't there, to search Tight End for the missing outer.

Waiting for the Crime Central forensic scientists to arrive, Troy looked up Zoe Olivia Three's address. As soon as two officers turned up at the jeweller's shop with their analytical kits, Troy directed them to the suspect's work space. Then he left for Zoe's apartment.

Troy glanced around the stylish living room and said, 'Where's Nigel Edwin Thirty-One?'

Taken by surprise, Zoe Three answered with a shrug. 'No idea. Not here. At work, I should think.'

'You don't deny knowing him?'

'No. Why should I?'

Zoe seemed full of confidence. She was about the same age as Troy and she had long dark hair – almost black. She had a bracelet on each wrist, gold earrings and an expensive necklace.

'What's your relationship with him?'

She shrugged again. 'We're friends.' With a strange little smile, she added, 'He seems to like me.'

'You go out together?'

'Yes. I don't think it's against the law.'

'That depends where you go and what you do. How about Loose End Edge?'

For the first time, she looked uncertain. 'I don't like to say.'

'Why not?'

'Well, it's full of lovely hidden places. I want to keep them to ourselves, not broadcast how good they are.'

'So, you do go there?'

'Good walking, picnic places, wild swimming in out-of-the-way pools.'

'That's why you've been seen starting out with big bags, then?'

'Guess so.'

'Have you seen anyone else up there?'

She shook her head. 'Maybe once or twice, but it's not bursting at the seams.'

'I see you've got a lot of jewellery.'

'Nigel works in a jeweller's. He likes to give me presents.'

'Gold.'

'Some of it, yes.'

'I've got a lot of evidence of illegal gold mining under Loose End Edge.'

Unconcerned, Zoe shrugged. 'Nothing to do with me.'

In the face of her bravado, Troy knew he was on weak ground. She had accounted for Shea Pickup's sighting of the couple at Loose End Edge and she had done so convincingly. Troy's only suspicion was that her body language and responses were too confident and convincing. Even innocent suspects hesitated and showed signs of weakness, anxiety and doubt. But being self-assured wasn't a crime. He had no justification for requesting a sample of her DNA.

'Okay,' he said. 'That all figures. Thanks for your time.'

'No problem,' she replied jauntily.

# SCENE 28

*Tuesday 13th May, Night*

'What have you got so far?' Troy asked his partner at Tight End Crime Central.

'That water looked unspoiled – ideal for wild swimming – but it's contaminated. Invisibly.'

'Mercury?'

'Yes. That's why the fish died downstream.' Lexi looked at him and said, 'I know exactly what happened. Somewhere around the pool – and the amateur mining operation – there was a big spillage of mercury. Here's the bad news. DNA profiling of the water tells me it's got bacteria – probably on the riverbed – that turn mercury into methylmercury. Hey presto. That's how and why fish and majors died. The bugs in the river are converting the pollution into the nastiest form of mercury.'

Troy nodded. 'What about the gear in the cave?'

'The two buckets had mercury in them. No fingerprints on anything. But I got hair and skin from the hard-hats. I'll have the DNA results in the morning. Till then, nothing's certain, but one hair was silvery and it looks like it matches the hair on Keaton Hathaway's pad.'

Troy smiled. 'Good work.'

'We'll see.'

'Anything else?'

'The fishing hook. I got a microscopic skin sample from it. That's in for DNA right now.'

Troy said, 'I've put some stuff in the forensic queue as well. Samples from a silver-haired, brown-eyed assistant at the jewellery shop in town. Nigel Edwin Thirty-One. An expert mineralogist and geologist. Friend of Zoe Three. Visitor to Loose End Edge.'

'Interesting. Have you set up surveillance on him?'

Troy paused. 'Horatio Vines told him I was after him. He took off. But there's a police team out looking for him. I don't think he's with Zoe. Which reminds me. Are any of the hairs on the helmets long and black?'

'Two of them.'

'We're going to need DNA from Zoe Olivia Three, then.'

# SCENE 29

*Wednesday 14th May, Early morning*

Over breakfast in his hotel, Troy examined the main results that Lexi had sent to his life-logger.

## DNA Profiles

✦ DNA from mushroom, *Rhodotus palmatus*, detected in wooded area by pool.

✦ DNA profile of Nigel Edwin Thirty-One established from hair and skin found in his working area of jewellery shop in Tight End.

✦ DNA from root of silver hair on hard-hat matches exactly with the DNA from the hair in Hathaway's notebook. Both are identical to the DNA profile of

Nigel Edwin Thirty-One.

+ DNA from root of dark hair on second hard-hat does not match with any profile in any database.

+ DNA from fishing hook matches post-mortem sample of Richard Featherstone.


Troy smiled to himself and fisted the air. Through the wrinkled peach and the wild-swimming map, he had good evidence that Miley Quist had visited the valley below Loose End Edge. She had probably had a swim in the poisoned pool and maybe drunk the water.

He also had certain evidence that Richard Featherstone had been in the same place. Horatio Vines had seen another victim, Alyssa Bending, with Richard. It seemed likely that they had caught and unknowingly eaten contaminated fish. Maybe they'd had a swim as well.

Troy had the crime scene, the weapon and a suspect he could place in the same area. Nigel Edwin Thirty-One probably used mercury to scavenge illegally for gold. He didn't have an obvious motive, though. He probably poisoned the victims by accident.

Troy also had undeniable evidence linking him with the fourth victim. Nigel Thirty-One had tried to destroy Keaton Hathaway's connection to Loose End Edge by removing the latest pages from his journal.

But did Nigel have an accomplice? Or an apprentice for his mining operation. Was Zoe Olivia Three involved?

It struck Troy that, if she was mixed up in the crime, she could have a motive for the killing. She wanted to keep the whole area to herself and Nigel. Was she so selfish that she was prepared to kill strangers who strayed into her precious playground?

Troy imagined that Lexi's scientific spreadsheet was telling the same story, highlighting the same connections. The rogue squirrels of Pickling were off the hook, for sure.

In a separate message, his life-logger told him that the whereabouts of Nigel Edwin Thirty-One were still unknown. 'He's not at home. More than that, he's nowhere to be seen. Search continuing.'

Another unknown was bothering Troy. Where did Nigel Thirty-One get mercury? The most obvious source was Tight End Recycling Facility just a few kilometres away, but Troy had no evidence for or against.

He sent a request to Caroline Seventeen and Jon Drago Five at TERF for a fresh and complete audit on all their mercury. Then he pushed away his empty plate, knocked back the remains of the strong coffee and set out for Tight End Crime Central.

# SCENE 30

On his way to the local police headquarters, Troy received a call from TERF's chief scientist. Caroline Seventeen told him, 'We're already conducting an audit of our mercury stock – at the request of Detective Lexi Iona Four. She emailed during the night.'

'Not sleeping has its advantages.'

'I'll have an answer for you later today but, to be honest, I can't conceive of any way our records could be in error by more than milligrams.'

'One other thing,' Troy said.

'What?'

'Have you come across Nigel Edwin Thirty-One or Zoe Olivia Three?'

'The names don't ring a bell. Just a moment.'

In the distance, Troy heard a faint siren, but he focussed on the phone call. He guessed that Caroline was searching a database.

A few seconds later, the chief scientist said, 'I have nothing on Nigel Edwin Thirty-One, but nearly a year ago a Zoe Olivia Three did some work experience here. She was competent, hard-working and keen according to my file, but this business wasn't glamorous enough for her, apparently. She didn't stay.'

'But she learned all the ins and outs of mercury recycling?'

'Yes.'

'In that case, I think you should double-check your on-site store of mercury because I *can* conceive of a way your records are wrong – if someone who knows her way around the factory sneaked in and took what she wanted.'

'I'll be in touch.'

'Thanks.'

The driverless car was approaching Tight End Crime Central and Troy felt a sudden chill down his spine. There were clusters of people standing outside the old building and thick grey smoke surged from its upper storeys. Through the windows, he could see the yellow flicker of flames. The ominous and urgent sound of sirens was getting louder. Even before the car came to a halt, Troy opened the door, jumped out and ran towards the building. Looking at the assembled staff, immediately he noticed that Lexi wasn't among them.

On his life-logger was a single word. *Trapped*. Without a thought about his own safety or his father's fate, Troy raced to the side-entrance of the forensic labs.

As soon as he went inside, he coughed. The air was acrid and sooty. The whole place was unnaturally hot, but the flames were further down the wooden corridor and on the floor above. Troy could hear alarms, sirens and worrying creaks and crashes.

He dashed towards the forensic department and, at the same time, placed a handkerchief over his nose and mouth, tying it tightly behind his head. He opened the door on the left and a blast of heat enveloped him. Patches of the large room were utterly black. Equipment along the far bench was scattered and ablaze. The main rafter supporting the storey above had fallen. It had pinned two chromatographs and Lexi Iona Four to the floor.

Troy dashed to his partner's side. The heavy oak beam had collapsed across Lexi's right leg. Both of them coughed as a section of plaster and a smaller wooden joist came down in a cloud of dust and hot ash. Above their heads, the floorboards were aflame. The whole ceiling was not going to stay up for long and when it gave way, they would be pelted with burning wreckage.

'Are you hurt?' Troy asked, almost shouting at her.

'I don't think so. Bruised, but I don't think anything's broken. I just can't shift the wood.'

Troy knew as soon as he put his arms round the beam and heaved that it was not going to budge. Even so, he tried twice more before giving up.

He looked down at Lexi's lower leg and foot poking out from the other side of the rafter and groaned. 'I think there might be a way.' He paused and asked, 'Is there a saw in here? You must have to saw into bits of evidence sometimes.'

Lexi gulped but nodded. 'A big hacksaw hooked on the wall. Over there.' She pointed. 'Facemasks on the bench as well.'

Troy jumped over some unidentifiable smouldering remains and grabbed the hacksaw. Its metal handle was warm. The ineffective handkerchief fell from his face. Behind him, some flaming timber dropped down and struck him on the back. He ignored the discomfort. He grasped two facemasks and fitted one over Lexi's mouth and nose. Then he pulled the other over his own face.

Again, he examined the beam and his partner's protruding leg. He knew he didn't have long and he couldn't see any other option. He would have to select the right place to cut very carefully. 'Okay. I'm going to try it,' he yelled. 'All right?'

Lexi winced and nodded.

'I think I know where's best to saw through.'

Lexi swallowed and shut her eyes.

Troy picked his spot, took a deep breath and began to pump the hacksaw back and forth. The teeth of the blade bit into the timber and began to make a thin groove.

Lexi opened her eyes again and gazed at Troy. She sighed. 'For a moment there I thought ... '

'What?'

'Nothing. Is it working?'

'It's not easy but I'll do it if it's the last thing ... ' He decided not to continue the sentence. 'I can't move the whole beam, but I reckon I'll shift half of it when I cut it in two.'

Troy put all his strength and concentration into sawing. He watched as each thrust and back-stroke went a few millimetres deeper into the timber. He sawed as fast as he could, using as much power as he possessed, thinking that would cut through the wood as quickly as possible.

Really, the hacksaw wasn't designed for slicing large chunks of timber, but it was Troy's only weapon. He was soon drenched in perspiration. The effort, the tension and the fiery heat made him sweat like a boxer. His right shoulder and arm began to ache – but he didn't slow. If anything, he attacked the oak even more, wanting to get it over with before his muscles gave up altogether. And before the ceiling gave way.

He could not rely on help arriving in time. He guessed that firefighters were outside, weighing up their options. Even if they'd entered the building, Troy thought they'd concentrate on the main offices and incidents rooms.

To his left, a large section of the ceiling caved in. He barely noticed the blazing floorboards spreading the fire. One whole laboratory bench was now well alight. The room was filling with toxic gases. Dark fumes gathered like menacing clouds above their heads.

Lexi cried out, 'It's not working. Save yourself.'

'Shush,' Troy gasped obstinately.

'The masks stop particles, not poison gas. You'll be overcome.'

A joist fell like a burning spear, just missing Troy.

'Save your breath.'

But Troy would be the first to succumb. Tiredness made him take great gulps of the toxic air.

Easing herself up on her elbows, Lexi watched her partner. The blade of the hacksaw was labouring through the last two centimetres of wood, but each stroke drained Troy of energy and made less impact on the timber.

'Nearly there,' Lexi shouted, encouraging him.

He had to finish the job, but his right arm was spent. He adjusted his stance and attacked the rafter with his left hand instead. His sawing action was awkward with that arm, but at least the teeth of the jagged blade sank more into the wood. Sawdust began to spray again as he pushed and pulled frenziedly.

The smell had become almost unbearable. The gases came from burning wood, fabric and plastic. They clung horribly to his mouth, throat and lungs.

Lexi put out an arm and slapped the trousers of his leg where the cloth brushed against a red-hot piece of fallen floorboard and caught fire. She put out the flames before they really got started.

Troy took no notice.

Then, the beam finally gave way. Troy thrust so hard at the final stroke that he nearly toppled over. He threw down the hacksaw and grabbed with both arms the part of the beam that lay over Lexi's leg. He bent his knees like a weight-lifter, steeled himself and heaved with all his remaining energy. Because he had exerted himself so much, the rafter did not shift.

After all that effort, though, he wasn't going to admit defeat. He refused to leave his partner to her fate. From somewhere, he had to summon more strength. Internally, he prayed for help, for a little intervention. Then he took a deep breath of foul air, gritted his teeth and strained every muscle to lift the beam. It didn't move much, but it was enough. Lexi squirmed out from under it and at once stood upright. She lurched and swayed but her leg held her weight.

Troy let go of the half-rafter but, nearing exhaustion, remained flat-out on the floor.

The room was shrouded in a thick poisonous fog. Lexi and Troy could barely see each other. The remaining part of the ceiling crashed down and rested on the benches. Lexi ducked down and grabbed Troy. Together, bent double, they crawled as quickly as they could out of the lab. They sprawled into the corridor, straight into the path of a firefighter.

The officer was wearing more protective gear than an astronaut. Neither Troy nor Lexi could tell if they'd stumbled into a man or a woman. But the firefighter helped them both up, propelled them rapidly down the corridor to the nearest exit and out into cool, fresh air.

The officer didn't allow them to flop onto the ground. Gripping an arm of each of them, the firefighter marched them away from the building that was in danger of collapse, dragging them to the assembly point. Only then did the officer release their arms and let them relax.

At once, Troy bent over, yanked the mask from his blackened face and vomited abundantly.

Normally so cool, calm and unemotional, Lexi gave in to her sense of relief and sobbed.

# SCENE 31

'How are you feeling?' Lexi asked.

'Like my throat and lungs are on fire,' Troy replied. 'They've been thoroughly sandpapered. What about you?'

They were sitting together next to Troy's hospital bed. On the tray in front of them were two meals – one major and one outer – but both detectives toyed with their food rather than tucked into it. The fire had taken away their appetites for minced meat and grasshopper salsa tacos.

'Black and blue but okay,' Lexi answered. 'They

scanned my whole body. Not a bone out of place. I have a beautiful, intact skeleton.' She paused before adding, 'What do you think it was all about?'

Troy knew she was referring to the fire. 'An accident, someone being careless in an old risky building, or someone deliberately trying to destroy evidence. Or us.'

Lexi nodded. 'If it was arson, it sort of worked. Our physical evidence has gone. I was trying to save it. That's why I lingered too long in the lab and got my leg squelched.' She sighed with regret. 'I'll never get to check when and where the hard-hats were bought, and who bought them. The central computer's died a death as well. Fried. And all the security cameras have melted or something. They're not working. We're not going to see who did it or what happened.'

'We only lost the back-up.' Troy tapped his life-logger. 'All the forensic details and your results are in here.'

'Might be able to salvage lots from mine as well,' said Lexi.

'And, if the idea was to get rid of us, it didn't work. Not quite.'

Lexi shuffled uncomfortably in her seat. 'I'm not good at this sort of thing,' she said, 'but you did something amazing this morning.'

'Did I?'

'Days after your dad … you know … you did the same. You ran into a fire. And you stayed with me, even when it looked bad. Thanks.'

Troy shrugged. 'I didn't fancy having to get used to a new partner.'

'Huh.'

A doctor came into the room and smiled at Troy. 'You're a lucky lad. You're free to go. You're nowhere near one hundred per cent, but what you need most is rest and fresh air. If you get dizzy or short of breath, relax or come back for more oxygen treatment. My best prescription is: take it easy. If you see anyone who needs rescuing, let somebody else do it. And don't go chasing bad guys.'

'Thanks.'

'Some chance,' Lexi whispered to herself.

Troy's life-logger vibrated with an incoming message from Jon Drago Five at Tight End Recycling Facility. Troy read it and then said to Lexi, 'TERF has got less mercury on site than they thought. They can only explain it if someone's been breaking in and nicking it.'

'No great surprise. I'll send a forensic team to check it out.'

Troy nodded. 'First stop after this is Zoe Three's place.'

# SCENE 32

*Wednesday 14th May, Afternoon*

Zoe Olivia Three was not at home. Standing by the front door, Troy looked at his partner and said, 'What do you think? Have we got enough on her to go in and take DNA without her permission?'

'She used to work at the place where the mercury comes from. The description of her hair matches what I found on one of the hard-hats. She's very friendly with our main suspect, Nigel Thirty-One. A witness says she's been with him to the crime scene. Yes, we can justify a break-in.'

'Give the door some welly,' Troy said.

As soon as Lexi's leg impacted with the wood, the door sprang back and Lexi let out a cry of pain. Smiling wryly, she said, 'Another bruise won't make much difference.'

While Lexi collected some skin and hair samples from Zoe's bedroom, their life-loggers received a photograph of two hooded people taken by a security camera on the property neighbouring Tight End Crime Central. One was holding the type of can used for carrying fuel.

Troy and Lexi both examined the sinister figures and came to the conclusion that they couldn't identify either. There weren't enough features on show. Even an advanced facial recognition program was unlikely to recognize them.

Straightaway, Lexi arranged for a police motorcyclist to collect the new evidence on Zoe Olivia Three and speed it as a priority to the nearest working forensic laboratory.

Troy called for an update on the team searching for Nigel Thirty-One. Because of the fire, there were few police officers to continue the hunt and they remained clueless.

Troy trickled cold blueberry juice past his sore throat and it eased the stinging sensation. Lexi swallowed a lot of beer and it did nothing at all for her aching leg.

'I'm thinking about where they might go,' said Troy.

'And?' Lexi prompted.

'I'm thinking about Loose End Edge.'

Lexi nodded slowly. 'Good point. If they spend quite a lot of time out there, it'll be a second home to them. Lots of secret places to hide away. And deserted, so they won't be seen.'

'Except they *will* be seen.' Troy raised his eyebrows. 'Won't they?'

'My spy camera! Yes, of course.' Fiddling with her life-logger, she said, 'I'll check – if it's still working after someone tried to barbeque it this morning.' She tapped on the keypad and sighed with frustration. 'There was some action on the camera, but my life-logger didn't record it properly.' She growled to herself. 'No movies but I've got some stills. Look. Two people about to go down the mineshaft in that cage.'

'Wearing the same clothes as our fire-starters.'

'Yeah. You're right.' The next snapshot that Lexi discovered showed their faces clearly. At once, she shared it with her partner.

Troy nodded. 'Nigel Edwin Thirty-One and Zoe Olivia Three.'

Lexi got to her feet but Troy didn't follow suit. She said, 'What's bothering you?'

'In a way, the fire was my fault.'

Puzzled, Lexi asked, 'How do you make that out?'

'I told Zoe we'd got evidence about gold-mining. She obviously decided to get rid of it.'

'Look. I've just seen two people with petrol heading towards Crime Central. I think I know who to blame – and it's not you,' Lexi replied. 'Come on. Time to organize another expedition.'

# SCENE 33

As they made their way to their separate positions, Troy and Lexi realized that they could be walking into a trap.

If Nigel Thirty-One and Zoe Three had spotted the spy camera at the head of the mineshaft, they could be luring the detectives back to Loose End Edge and another ambush.

'First kill the evidence and then kill us,' Troy said into his microphone.

'If the fire didn't finish us off.'

'Exactly.'

'Are you having second thoughts about this?' asked Lexi.

'No. Not really.'

'Good,' Lexi replied, 'Because there's only one way to find out – and that's by doing what we're doing.'

Troy agreed. 'If they didn't spot the camera, that's where they'll be hiding and we'll have to flush them out.'

'Agreed. We keep to the plan.'

They were in radio contact at all times, but part of two different units. Lexi was leading a group of four fit and healthy volunteers to the mouth of the cave. They were all outers and they had rope ladders to help them ascend the rock to the pool. Troy was in a car with three other police officers. They would soon arrive at the top of the shaft with the pulley and basket. At first, they planned to wait there in case Lexi's team drove Nigel and Zoe successfully towards the hole, until there was nowhere for the two suspects to go but upwards. If that didn't happen, though, Troy's crew would go down and join the others in the cave. Troy and one officer would descend in the basket first, followed by the other two.

Before the car reached its destination, Troy made the final arrangements through his life-logger and mobile phone.

When they arrived, he talked to Lexi again using the microphone attached to his coat. 'In position,' he reported. 'What about you?'

Through his earpiece, she said, 'Skirting round the pool, trying not to fall in the water or down the rock. We'll be ready any second now.'

'Watch out for sabotage or whatever.'

With humour and barely a trace of nervousness in her voice, she replied, 'We're going into a mine. What could possibly go wrong?'

'You're right. It's not like you're going to come across anything dangerous like pickaxes, unstable rocks, explosives ... '

'If you're ready up there, we're going in.'

Troy looked around. Soon, they would lose all remnants of sunlight. For now, the sky provided a faint and eerie orange glow. He shivered. He didn't know if he felt uneasy because of his injuries, the plunging temperature or uncertainty about what they were doing. 'Ready,' he said.

Five high-power torches cast wavering beams of light into the cavity. Addressing her team, Lexi asked, 'Are we all okay with this?'

'Yes.'

She glanced around their patchily lit faces. 'The

only people I want with me are ones who fancy it. You're all volunteers. You're free to go if you want.'

None of them made a move.

'Good. Keep a lookout for anything. This isn't just about finding two people. It's about finding anything they might have left behind if they're not here. Okay? I don't mind how many false alarms we have. We stop for anything remotely suspicious. We all know what they're capable of.' She didn't need to explain that she was referring to the destruction of the local police headquarters.

Cautiously, they stepped inside and began to creep along the rough tunnel in the rock face. To Lexi, it felt even more suffocating and smelly this time. The extra light helped, but it was also off-putting. An officer behind her would catch her figure in a light beam and her elongated silhouette would dance uncannily down the cave. There was more illumination but there were also more unexpected shadows. More unnerving movements. And the odd noise from the rest of the squad made them all jittery.

In Lexi's ear, Troy's voice asked, 'Still receiving me?'

'This is where I normally say no,' Lexi whispered, 'but I don't feel in the mood for joking.'

'Are you all okay down there?'

'Yeah. Having a picnic. Nothing to report yet.'

Two torch beams focused on the few tools that Lexi had left behind last time. 'No,' she whispered. 'I know about them. Crack on.'

Then she halted. Behind her, the others did the same.

'Did anyone else hear that?'

'What?'

'I don't know. Like a pulse. A beating.'

It was obvious that Lexi was the only one to pick out the sound. Or maybe it was her imagination.

They carried on slowly, heading towards the hole in the roof of the cave.

'Here's something.' At least three of the spotlights converged on a can of fuel.

Lexi edged towards it, but didn't attempt to reach out and touch it. Into her microphone, she said softly, 'A can of petrol. Probably empty.' To her team, she said, 'We want this. We'll come back for it but no one goes up to it now. We can't be sure it's not booby-trapped.'

Creeping as quietly as possible, the team walked through a watery section of the cavity as it began to rise up gently. Lexi thought that the vertical shaft would be visible soon, but there was no tell-tale sunshine this time to reveal its position.

A tiny glinting in the wall of the cave hinted at its potential for yielding gemstones and minerals. But Lexi wasn't drawn to jewellery. She was focused entirely on the case, the hunt for two clear suspects.

One beam of light caught the distant dangling rope and another picked out a discarded box of matches in the middle of the passageway.

'Some matches, now,' Lexi muttered for Troy's benefit.

'I'm worried,' Troy said directly into her ear.

'Why?'

'In case someone's laid a trail. Like bits of cheese to get a mouse to go where you want it to go.'

'Noted.'

With a wave of a finger, Lexi indicated to her team that she wanted to continue.

She managed four more steps before she froze. 'I'm sure I can hear something. Not trickling water. Something else.'

Behind her, someone said, 'Me too.'

There was definitely a strange distant rushing noise.

It didn't remain distant. The sound soon amplified. Something or someone was thundering ominously along the cave.

In Lexi's ears, it was as obvious and deadly as a train. She dived to the ground. Behind her, the rest of the team did the same.

Above them, hundreds and hundreds of bats surged through the foul air, wings fluttering, eager to begin their nightly hunt over the valley.

Lying still on the wet rock, Lexi told Troy, 'It's okay. Just bats. Billions of them.'

And that was the last thing she said. Further along the cave, one bat flew into the tripwire intended for human beings. It triggered a massive explosion.

At the top of the shaft, the four police officers stepped back from the hole and covered their faces. The shockwave smashed the cage against the winch and shattered it. Fragments of the basket, stones, dead bats, and clouds of dust blasted into the night air. Rope flew out of the hole like a snake. It seemed that an angry Earth was spewing out parts of itself.

Then the debris rained down on them like hailstones. One officer cried out as a bat's body hit his neck and shoulder. In seconds, though, it was over. Only a grey haze hung over the mineshaft, like smoke mushrooming over an exhausted volcano.

Troy put his hand to his earpiece and strained to hear the slightest suggestion of a human voice. It didn't come. There were three thuds and nothing else. He turned off the microphone.

After the initial shock, one of the police officers made for the jeep, clearly intending to call for ambulances. But Troy called softly, 'No. Come back. We're all going to lie down here and not make a sound.'

'What?'

'I want the suspects to think they've succeeded. If we're all dead, there's no one to call an ambulance.'

They followed Troy's example and laid themselves on the rocky ground but one of them complained, 'What about the others?' He tapped his own ear while nodding towards Troy's. 'Have you heard anything?'

Troy shook his head. 'Radio silence. In case anyone's hacked us and is listening in.'

'But they need help.'

'No,' Troy replied. 'They're okay. Lexi gave me the signal. Three taps on the microphone. They're playing dead. Like us. Now keep quiet and still, but listen and watch.'

Every single road in the area was blocked by the police. Out at sea, a boat was patrolling the coast. Northern harbours and train stations were under surveillance. Both airports serving the north of the country were on high alert. This clampdown was what Troy had arranged during his ride to Loose End Edge.

If he didn't catch Nigel Edwin Thirty-One and Zoe Olivia Three on Loose End Edge, he hoped that one of the transport units would conclude the arrest.

Nigel Thirty-One and Zoe Three emerged from nowhere, it seemed. Zoe held a torch and flashed it at each of the four victims lying near the top of the shaft. Without a word of regret, they weaved their way among the dead and glanced down the concealed mineshaft. Directing the torch beam down the hole, Zoe said, 'What a mess.'

'But it's over,' Nigel replied. 'They're gone.'

The couple exchanged a self-satisfied smile and a kiss. Then they turned to go and jumped in fright.

In front of them, Detective Troy Goodhart said, 'Not entirely gone.'

Nigel stiffened with shock – and possibly humiliation. Zoe made a run for it. She didn't get far. One of Troy's team stayed low and brought her down gleefully with a perfectly executed rugby tackle.

Troy turned on his microphone again and said, 'Two arrested on suspicion of arson and attempted murder.

Are you all okay down there?'

At first there was no response, but then Lexi replied, 'How many bruises do I have to get before I'm classed as not okay?'

Troy sighed with relief. The sound of his partner's voice was priceless. 'North of what you've got, I should think. What about the others?'

'All walking wounded. A couple of nasty cuts from flying lumps of rock – and more bruises. Lucky we were lying down at the time – and nowhere near the source of the blast.' She hesitated. 'You know, I have a newfound respect for bats. They're great. And I don't care how much toileting they do, how they do it and how smelly it is.'

Troy laughed. 'See you soon.'

# SCENE 34

*Thursday 15th May, Morning*

Troy had refreshed himself with a long, sound sleep at home in Shepford. Lexi had meditated much more than usual in an attempt to heal her aching body. In between periods of relaxation, she'd had the two prisoners transported separately to Shepford Crime Central and examined the latest forensic results from Zoe Three's home. By dawn, she was ready to support her partner as he attempted to close the case.

Troy decided to question Nigel Thirty-One first because he was probably the weaker of the two characters. In a sparse interview room, Troy sat opposite the silver-haired suspect as Lexi prowled back and forth.

'You should know before we begin,' Troy said, hoping to demoralize the geologist, 'that I'm going to charge you with a minimum of two crimes. I've got all the evidence I need. And that's before we think about what you did last night. You're not going to get up and walk out of here after our chat.'

Nigel sneered. 'You're bluffing. You've got no evidence.'

'What makes you say that?'

'Because I heard there was a fire.'

Troy put a hand to his ear theatrically. 'I can't hear the sound of wheels coming off this line of inquiry.' He gazed at Nigel and said, 'You don't understand how it works. You destroyed the physical evidence all right but – you should know better than me – outers work around the clock. Lexi and a whole bunch of forensic scientists found out lots before you burned the place down. The results are still valid even if the evidence has turned to ash. And, yes, one of the charges will be arson. Tight End Crime Central isn't the only place that has cameras.'

'I still think you're bluffing. I bet the computer's not working.'

'You're right. It's not,' Troy told him. 'But the same

information's stored on the life-loggers of all detectives working on the case.' He tapped the device attached to his waist. 'I've got a copy and Lexi's life-logger survived almost intact. Believe me, the best you can hope for are charges of arson and attempted murder.'

Nigel folded his arms tightly across his chest.

'Why did you poison Richard Featherstone, Alyssa Bending, Miley Quist and Keaton Hathaway?'

'I didn't,' Nigel stated bluntly. 'No way. You've got the wrong end of the stick.'

'Why did you tear some pages out of Keaton Hathaway's diary?'

'It's funny you should mention him.'

'Is it?'

'Yes. Because he's the man you want. He came to Loose End, volunteered to work with us and got overexcited. Stupid. He spilled a whole load of mercury into the pool. Nearly put us out of business. That's how people got poisoned. Nothing to do with us.'

Troy barely reacted to Nigel's revelation. He merely raised his eyebrows. 'When you say us, do you mean you and Zoe Olivia Three?'

'Yes.'

'Tell me about Zoe. What part did she play in all this?'

He shrugged. 'She helps me.'

'She's an equal partner?'

'You could say that.'

'And will she confirm what you just said about Keaton Hathaway?'

'I don't see why not.'

Troy stood up. 'I'll go and find out.'

On the other side of the main corridor through Shepford Crime Central, Zoe Olivia Three sat bolt upright, oozing confidence. There was an ugly bruise and graze on the left side of her face where her head had hit the rock as she tried to evade arrest.

Troy pointed to her wound and asked, 'Are you satisfied you've had enough medical treatment for that?'

She stared at him maliciously but said nothing.

'I'll take it that you're happy with it. Do you play a full part in Nigel Thirty-One's gold-mining business?'

'No. He does it, not me.'

'So, if he blamed you for poisoning people with mercury … ?'

'What? He's lying.'

Troy put up a hand. 'I didn't say he did. I was just wondering. Do you do any mining at all, then?'

'No. Nothing to do with me.'

'Where does he get mercury from?'

She shrugged.

'What about Tight End Recycling Facility?'

She shrugged again.

'Didn't you work there?'

'For a bit.'

'So, you'd know where they keep a stock of it.'

She didn't reply.

'You supplied him with it. There's a forensic team in TERF, so we'll soon prove it.'

'I had nothing to do with digging for gold,' she insisted.

If Troy didn't know better, he might have been convinced by her performance. He twisted round towards his partner. 'Lexi?'

'We have samples of your hair,' she said. 'It matches two hairs we found on one of the helmets. Same colour, same DNA profile.'

Troy added, 'I don't think hard-hats are in fashion right now, so how do you explain that? Why have you been wearing one?'

'Can you show it to me?'

'No. It was mangled in the fire.'

'There you are, then. You can't prove anything.'

'We've got close-ups of the hair in the helmet. Very

clear photographic evidence. We've got DNA profiles. They don't go away when you destroy the evidence. And we have your activities last night. So it's easy for us to show you were part of the mining operation.'

This time, she kept silent.

'Tell me. Who murdered Richard Featherstone, Alyssa Bending, Miley Quist and Keaton Hathaway?'

'Not me,' Zoe muttered.

Troy smiled. 'That's what Nigel said as well. *Not me.*'

Her expression became even more stony. 'Are you saying he blamed me?'

'Who was it?'

'Keaton Hathaway himself. He was after gold and some other rocks. Not the tidiest man in the world.'

'How do you know that?'

'Because ... '

'Because you worked alongside Nigel and Keaton – in your hard-hat. That's how you know.'

Her lips sealed tightly once more.

'What did Keaton do to make you blame him?'

'He knocked over a whole bucketful of mercury. Incredibly heavy. I don't know how he could, but he did. It went everywhere – including all over him – but most of it would've ended up in the pool. Anyway, he had too much for a major.'

'Did you tell him to go to hospital?'

She shook her head. 'He wouldn't have listened. He carried on working, looking for gold, till he was too ill. Then he went home.'

'Are you sure?'

She did not answer.

'Lexi tells me mercury itself isn't dangerous if it doesn't get inside a major's body. It'd have to be injected or the vapour breathed in.'

'Maybe Hathaway breathed too much of it.'

'Are you sure you didn't force it into him as some sort of punishment?'

She stared directly at Troy. 'You're wrong. I already told you what happened. He poisoned himself, silly man.'

'Why did Nigel trash some of Keaton Hathaway's journal?'

'We knew he was going to die. Nigel just wanted to make sure no one traced him back to Loose End.'

Troy stood up. 'All right. I've got the picture. Not the whole picture, but I'm ready. I'm going to bring Nigel in and tell you both what's going to happen.'

Troy and Lexi sat shoulder-to-shoulder. On the opposite side of the table, Nigel Edwin Thirty-One and Zoe Olivia Three waited, eager to hear that someone else was going to be held responsible for the four deaths.

The light coming in through the window faded rapidly as if a huge storm was about to hit Shepford. Inside, the interview room suddenly seemed cold and dark. In the sky, the circle of the moon fitted precisely over the sun, blocking out its light and warmth.

Lexi turned on the lamp. 'Solar eclipse today. Only for a few minutes.'

Troy remained focused. He took a deep breath. 'Okay. You've both told me the same story. Independently. A clumsy Keaton Hathaway killed four people. One of them was himself.'

Nigel and Zoe smiled at each other.

'Of course, it's an easy claim for the two of you to make. He's dead. He can't paint me a different picture. But I'm inclined to believe the basic idea. It fits. In ripping up his journal you were protecting your business. There are still some parts I'm not sure about. Like what happened after the mercury got spilt. Why didn't Keaton get medical help? He was obsessive about rocks and things, so maybe he was too keen on finding gold to stop. Maybe he carried on working, thinking he was safe, not realizing the local river life was turning the mercury into something deadly for majors. Maybe he took too much mercury on-board trying to clear up his own mess. I don't know what he was really like. Maybe he would have left, but you two didn't let him. Maybe you poisoned him deliberately. I don't know and I can't trust either of you to tell me. But I agree that one of the victims was the culprit.'

In another mini-celebration, Nigel and Zoe exchanged a triumphant grin.

Troy leaned forward. 'Time to burst your balloon. Even if every word you've said is true,' Troy told them, 'you're guilty of multiple killing.'

Their mood changed instantly. 'What?' they both cried.

'You knew Keaton Hathaway would die if he carried on. He was a major. You didn't get medical help because you were more interested in saving your income. You could have come forward straightaway, admitted what happened and the whole place would've been sealed off and dealt with. The only casualties would have been fish and a few birds or whatever. Keaton Hathaway would probably have got sick and recovered. But, no, you caused death by neglect, by not coming forward. All because you didn't want to admit to a mining racket. For that, four people died. You thought four majors weren't as important as a few scraps of gold.' Troy banged the table top angrily. 'You're responsible for those deaths. You're both as big a killer as Keaton Hathaway.'

At the window, a blaze of sunlight announced the end of the brief eclipse.

# SCENE 35

Lexi waved a skewer of crispy scorpions at her partner. 'Nicely handled, 'she said.

'Isn't that poisonous?' Troy pointed at her meal.

'Not after cooking,' Lexi replied. 'Neither are stir-fried bean sprouts, peanuts and lime.'

Troy pulled a face and chomped some more chocolate.

'I checked what Yasmin Nadya One said at the insect farm and she's right.'

'Oh?'

Lexi reminded him. 'You're eating bits of insects

right now. The maker's allowed up to sixty fragments in every hundred grams of chocolate.'

Troy smiled. 'That's different. Chocolate doesn't have legs and a head that needs snapping off.'

Lexi thought for a moment and then said, 'We've gone a long way. From north to south and squirrels to miners.'

'And victim to culprit.'

'Yeah.'

Lexi's phone rang and, when she answered it, the commander's voice said, 'You're wanted. You and Detective Troy Goodhart. I'm sending you the details now.'

'What is it?'

'There's been a car crash.'

Mystified, Lexi replied, 'We don't do car crashes.'

'You'll do this one.'

'Why?'

'Wait till you see what's in the back of it.'

'What?'

'Blood and bone – and much more besides.'

'Okay,' said Lexi. 'Now it does sound like one of ours.' She ended the call and smiled at Troy. 'He says thanks for solving another case. You did brilliantly. Take a well-earned holiday to recover and some time to feel pleased with yourselves.'

'Oh yeah?'

'Well, no. But let's finish the food at least. Sounds like we're going to need strong stomachs.'

# The real science behind the story

The crimes in all of *The Outer Reaches* books are inspired by genuine scientific issues and events. Here are a few details of the science that lies behind *Fatal Connection*.

## *Mercury in seafood*

A tragedy in Minamata, a fishing town in Japan, alerted the world to chemical contamination. In the 1940s, birds, pets and people began to lose control of their movements – a sign of brain damage. Almost half of the sick people died and women gave birth to dreadfully deformed children. Several hundred people died of 'Minamata disease' through the 1950s and 1960s. The town's biggest employer – a chemical company – had dumped a sludge containing mercury substances in Minamata Bay. The poisonous mercury had accumulated inside the fish and they had been eaten by the local population. Compensation claims almost bankrupted the chemical company and that convinced similar companies to take pollution seriously and clean up their acts. Cynics might say they were protecting their businesses from expensive pay-outs as much as protecting the public.

Today, the mercury pollution problem is not of Minamata proportions. But pregnant women with low levels of mercury in their bodies give birth to children who, in intelligence tests, lag behind their friends who had less contaminated mothers. Most people get more mercury from amalgam fillings in their teeth than from eating polluted fish, but the mercury from fillings is a far less toxic form.

Malcolm Rose is an established, award-winning author, noted for his gripping crime/thriller stories – all with a solid scientific basis.

Before becoming a full-time writer, Malcolm was a university lecturer and researcher in chemistry.

He says that chemistry and writing are not so different. *'In one life, I mix chemicals, stew them for a while and observe the reaction. In the other, I mix characters, stir in a bit of conflict and, again, observe the outcome.'*